WHY GOD WHY

I0527866

RESTORATION OF THE BREACH
WITHOUT BORDERS

LEOSTONE MORRISON

WHY GOD WHY?

Copyright © 2022 LEOSTONE MORRISON

All rights reserved. No part of this publication may be reproduced, copied, stored in a retrieval system, transmitted, scanned in any form or under any conditions, including, photocopying, electronic, recording, or otherwise, without the written permission of the author, Leostone Morrison.

ISBN: 978-1-954755-25-3

Published by:
Restoration of the Breach without Borders

West Palm Beach, Florida 33407

restorativeauthor@gmail.com

Tele: (561) 388-2949

Cover Design by:
Leostone Morrison

Editor: Juan Pablo
juanpablo_20@hotmail.com

Formatting and Publishing done by:
Sherene Morrison
Publisher.20@aol.com

REVIEWS

Why God? Why?" is carefully thought out and penned to paper. It gives inside details of the challenges that human beings are faced with daily. What I like about this book is the fact that you need no prior knowledge of these horrific situations to understand what actually is taking place in the real world because they have all been carefully and strategically decorated on each and every page. You are never able to predict what will happen next. It just keeps you at the edge of your chair, waiting for the mysteries to unfold.

The language employed throughout the entire script is emotive. From start to finish you will be emotionally charged. Happy, sad, frustrated, you name it. These emotions and more will be experienced as you take the journey of reading this book. I give the Why God Why? a 5 out of 5. I enjoyed the many nuggets to take away. For example, never wear your heart on your sleeve, always be aware of your surroundings and exercise wisdom always. I do believe this book will be a continuous series for years to come and I will be very pleased when it actually become a movie.

It's a must that you get your copy today and be a part of the rich legacy that is being created.

-Remone Benjamin Gordon
Author
(ABC of Grace)

This engaging story sheds light on the difficult decisions individuals have to make and the reality that faces them as they face the consequences of their choices. The Journey of this young lady involves a lot of reflecting and questioning in retrospect of her decision-making process. Why God Why is full of suspense as it dares to traverse different perspectives and scenes which opens our eyes to our own realities and those taboo and tough challenges faced especially by married couples that most are afraid to address.

-Esther Sinclair
Author
TRUTH 101

PART 1

"This is not true! It cannot be real!" exclaimed Marcia a wife of just two hours. The moment she anticipated since the age of fifteen was finally here, but it was saturated with disappointment. She fasted and prayed and got several confirmations from men and women of God regarding her husband. She had no doubt that God orchestrated their union. As they dated and planned their wedding, the favor of God was evident. God repeatedly demonstrated that this is His will for their lives.

Now it all made sense. The sexual purity enforced by her fiancé during their period of dating, was not merely about being in a right standing with God. It was a means of deception. Many questions flooded her mind. What should she do now? Should she live a lie for the rest of her life, or should she terminate the will of God? Were they deceived by evil spirits? Was this a plot by the ministers to destroy her happiness? Did God really truly love her? If He did, why have this evil been given to her? *Why, God Why?*

Marcia has struggled with her own identity from an early age. Her mother, Ruth, succumbed to HIV when she was 10 years old, but she had lost her to prostitution long before that. She has never met her father. Most likely he was one of her mother's many customers. Her mom grew up in a family living way below the poverty line, so she did not have the luxury of going to school regularly. Instead, Ruth often accompanied her mom, Lorna, to the market to help her sell vegetables. This is where she was introduced to one of the world's oldest professions at the tender age of fourteen. Selling her body seemed more lucrative than selling vegetables.

Ruth's way of making a living was killing her. She was raped several times by customers who demanded service without payment. On one occasion she was brutally beaten and stabbed multiple times and left for dead. The doctors said it was a miracle she survived. Even after that she stayed in the business. She was reckless. Ruth offered vaginal sex without protection to clients who did not want to wear condoms. Consequently, she became pregnant multiple times. Each time, she resolved it with an abortion.

Marcia was a failed abortion attempt. When Ruth realized that she was still pregnant, it was too advanced for another procedure. She went into antenatal depression and despised her baby. She refused to attend pre-natal clinic or to refrain from her trade. Interestingly, during her pregnancy, she saw an increase in clientele. Apparently, there are men who are excited by a pregnant prostitute. She was the envy of her competitors. After Marcia was born, her grandmother took her, and raised her as her own.

Not long after, Ruth met Dave, a pilot. He was so smitten by her abilities that he decided to marry her. After the wedding, she relocated from the tiny island of Bequia to join her newlywed in America. There she lived the good life. Dave insisted on her improving herself academically. He assisted her in not just getting her G.E.D but also putting her through college. Ruth graduated with a bachelor's degree with honors in Business Administration. She did not forget about her mother and daughter back home, as she would send them money regularly. However, visiting them was always just a broken promise.

Having gained her qualifications, she was able to secure an entry level position at a prominent insurance company. She was an industrious worker and would stay at the office after hours. In just a year, she was promoted to supervisor of the sales department. But there was a secret. She was selling more than just insurance. Ruth was sleeping with the boss, Mr. Harding. They thought that their incognito escapades were very subtle as no one in the office seemed to notice a thing.

However, unbeknownst to them, Mrs. Harding hired a private investigator who followed them around for two months. So, when the extramarital affair was made public, there was a barrage of evidence against them. On the day of the exposure, she ensured that she invited Dave to the office. He simply watched on as a spectator when Mrs. Harding, a sturdy woman, pummeled slim fit Ruth. He was ashamed, disappointed, embarrassed. Although he met her as a prostitute, he thought that their time together had somehow changed her. He requested an immediate divorce. Two months later, she was on a plane homebound without her pilot.

Back home. Single and broke. Not surprisingly, there was no reception party to greet her at the airport. She did not notify her mother of her situation. Ruth was too ashamed to go back to her community. How could she go back after the spectacular wedding she had on display? So, she decided to stay in the city. Certain of her qualification, she tried to find employment in various businesses. However, Ruth was repeatedly rejected. Finally, on the seventh interview, the manager explained why she was constantly denied a job. He informed her that most companies did a background check that included checking the applicant's social media accounts. There were still traces of her life as a prostitute circulating on Facebook available for public viewing.

Chris, the manager, claimed, "I believe in persons changing their lives for the better, but we have a reputable company's name that I must protect. Therefore..." Ruth cut him off with her wailing and begging, "please, please, please…" He got her to calm down. After a glass of water and wiping her snotty nose, she begged him to give her an opportunity once again. Chris sat pensive for a bit and then his face contorted as he made a fiendish smile. He offered her the job with the conditions of her deleting her Facebook account and being his personal call girl. She readily agreed.

Chris assisted her with a new wardrobe, getting an apartment and a company car. Ruth was an industrious worker and everyone on the team was happy to have her on board. She went beyond the call of duty. The arrangement with Chris was also going great. That is until he began altering it. He started inviting his rich executive friends over to her apartment for group sex. First it was one, but then the numbers increased. This adversely affected her work performance. She was too tired to focus on her work, so she started making simple errors. The company confiscated the car. Chris even threatened to fire her if she did not pull up her socks. However, after Ruth was exposed to cocaine at one of the house parties, she was immediately addicted. Additionally, she became an alcoholic. She once showed up to work wearing sunglasses and slept at her desk for hours.

Chris advised her to resign, and she took him up on the offer, as he also promised to take care of her.

Of course, taking care of her meant that he would be her pimp. She was back to being a full-time prostitute. Chris no longer had intimate relationships with her. He sold her services to the night's highest bidder. She knew her craft well and he exploited it. One of the richer clients, decided he wanted her for two months and paid the demand from Chris. He was dying and she did not know it. Whether Chris knew or not, remains unanswered. What is for certain is that she contracted HIV during her time with the terminally ill man. Chris then promptly ended their 'friendship' and evicted her from the apartment.

Lorna was cooking when she got the dreaded call from the main public hospital in the city. She was notified that a young lady gave her name and number as her emergency contact. She was dying and requested her mother to come quickly. The glass she had in her hand fell and shattered while the tears and scream flowed uncontrollably. Her only child was dying. She hurried to the city and seeing the state of her daughter lying limp on the hospital bed, she fainted. After recovery, she asked if she could take Ruth home. Lorna wanted her to spend her final days around persons who loved her. The doctors agreed and released Ruth to her mother's care. The journey home was quiet except for the soft sobbing that Lorna was desperately trying to suppress.

Outside of sick and dying, depression and regret consumed Ruth by the minute. The poverty that she desperately tried to escape had caught up to her. The pit toilet, zinc kitchen, wooden floor and kerosene lamp was still the home reality. As she laid on the makeshift bed, her life flashed before her. She once had expensive clothes, attended the best parties, and was acquainted with some of the wealthiest men. She was married to a pilot, lived in America, had a beautiful apartment and a company car. Now she is laying on old shoddy clothes and cardboards in a hastily erected zinc and board room extension to the house.

Marcia was not permitted to see her mom. This was painful for her. She had always been an obedient child, but she decided to disobey her grandmother with regards to this one thing. So, she secretly visited her mother. It was a visit of weeping! Her mother's first words to her were, "Who are you?" Her own flesh and blood mother did not recognize her. She stuttered while explaining that she was her daughter. During her speaking, her mother's bowels became loosened, and she soiled herself. Marcia decided to clean her although she sobbed quietly throughout the ordeal.

After cleaning her mother, they began talking about life. Marcia thanked her for all the financial help that she had sent throughout the years and expressed how overjoyed she was to finally meet her. Ruth apologized for not being there for her and lamented that she had wasted her life in vain pursuits. She recalled that her happiest moments had been singing hymns on the children's choir at church. They bonded over their mutual love for singing, and even sang a couple of hymns together. Ruth confessed that she had asked Jesus into her life at the age of eight. She said she loved God and prayed often while growing up. However, she had not prayed in a long time. Ruth asked Marcia if she knew how to pray- she said yes. During the shared time together, Ruth repented and recommitted her life to God.

Marcia secretly visited her mother for three months. She was with Ruth when she breathed her last on that unforgettable rainy Tuesday afternoon. Her mom had finally entered her life. She had waited so long for her. They were speaking every day. But now she was leaving her again. *'Why, God why?'* Marcia wondered why He would give her this joy, only to take it away so quickly.

The community did not attend Ruth's funeral. The community ostracized Marcia's family out of ignorance and fear of HIV. Marcia was banned from school. Fortunately, the principal, Mr. Parker, attended the same church as Grandma Lorna and was fond of

Marcia. He organized for her to do online schooling. Unfortunately, the isolation only added to the stifling grief of losing her mother. Marcia found comfort in knowing that her mother had given her life to Christ near the end.

Another challenge that they faced was getting provisions. The local shops and market vendors refused to do business with them. Thankfully, one of Grandma Lorna's friends from another community volunteered to buy and deliver the much-needed foods and supplies. He made sure to get essentials such as Kerosene oil, toilet paper and matches apart from the food items. He also sold Lorna's vegetables for her, as the community was also boycotting her at the marketplace. The proceeds from the sales were able to cover the expenses.

Marcia was tested for HIV four times within a six-month period and each time the reports came back negative. She was finally allowed to return to school and the shops and community reopened to them. One day, Marcia came home from school early and was shocked to hear the wailing sounds of someone in agony. It was her grandmother. She ran towards her in haste, but the bedroom door was locked. Grandma was finally crying the loss of her only child.

CHAPTER

2

To say it was challenging is an understatement. Marcia determined not to tread the path that her mother walked. She was baptized at the age of thirteen and became involved in the programs at her local church. All her grades were excellent except for Mathematics. Her neighbor, Ms. Clarke, was a teacher and volunteered to assist her whenever she was available. One day as she waited for her to get home for their scheduled session, her nineteen-year-old son, Anthony, raped her. He intimidated her into silence.

Anthony had forced her to do oral sex and used his phone to record her. He showed it to her and threatened to expose it if she ever told anyone. Moreover, he used the video to coerce her to frequently perform oral sex on him. After a while she became numbed and adjusted her mind to her new reality. One day he invited his best friend and demanded that she go down on him as well. When she refused, they both beat her.

Around that time, her church had two weeks of outreach programs. A few missionaries from America and Canada were present to assist with the work. Magrel, one of the younger visitors, was quickly drawn to Marcia. They spent copious amounts of time conversing and working together. After finding out about Marcia's mom, Magrel prayed on it and spoke to her husband, and then decided to ask Grandma Lorna if she could adopt Marcia. Her grandmother said yes. Magrel went back to Canada and commenced the procedure of adopting her.

The thought of leaving her grandmother was bittersweet for Marcia. Grandma Lorna was the one who raised her, and she knew she loved her. But Marcia was looking forward to escaping her community and not being around Anthony anymore. Three weeks before the approval of the adoption and travel documents were finalized, her grandmother passed away. Lorna spent the night praying and worshipping God, and then went to sleep. The following morning, she was unusually late from getting out of bed. When Marcia went in to check on her, she was dead. She passed in her sleep. Marcia was devasted. She felt paralyzed, defeated, and empty. Marcia was now motherless, fatherless, and granny-less. She cried herself to sleep that night hoping to wake up and find out that it was all a dream.

The funeral expenses were covered by the church and her grandmother was buried beside her daughter. The pastor said, she is at a better place. One where there is no more pain, tears or sorrow. Marcia was happy to hear those words. At the repass, Ms. Clarke offered to let her stay at her house until the missionary came for her. What Ms. Clarke thought was a gesture of kindness was rejected with a tsunami of rage. Marcia emptied her bowels to all who were present of the wickedness that Anthony had committed against her. They were completely shocked. The young man received a stern look from the local police chief who was a friend of the deceased. His mother seeing the look and knowing that he had recently applied to the police force, jumped to his defense, "Liar, liar, liar!" she shouted at Marcia. In the end, the pastor took her in until missionary Magrel returned for her.

It was not hard saying goodbye to her tattered pieces of clothing that Magrel advised her to leave behind. This was her first time at an airport, and the new clothes she wore made the event more memorable. Marcia, fifteen years old at the time, felt as though she was smiled upon by God. She allowed herself to dream of a beautiful future. They checked in and went through customs and she casually followed Magrel to a beautiful restaurant on the inside. She was not familiar with the names on the menu. Thus, she asked Magrel to order for her. The food looked nice and somehow tasted far better than it looked. She tried her best not to eat fast, especially since the couple beside them were acting as though they were more interested in talking than eating.

They boarded the plane. Magrel offered Marcia the window seat, but she politely declined. During takeoff, she held onto Magrel's hand, closed her eyes, and prayed earnestly. The food on the plane was not much better than what she was accustomed to at home, and definitely not in the same class as the food from the restaurant. Although she had a strong urge to urinate, she refused to unbuckle the seat belt. So, she held it for the duration of the flight. The plane experienced mild turbulence and Marcia screamed so loudly that an air hostess came running. Magrel comforted and reassured her that everything was okay. She tried to get Marcia to look at the clouds through the window, but once again the teen refused to utilize the window. Marcia just wanted to be back on the ground. They landed in Ontario, Canada and all Marcia could think was, *WOW*. To her the environment looked superb. *So, this is foreign,* she thought.

Magrel's husband, Sam, greeted them at the airport. Magrel introduced them, "Marcia, this is your dad. Mr. Martin, meet your new daughter." Marcia was happy to call Magrel mom, but it would take a while before she was comfortable seeing Sam as a dad. A beautiful black Mercedes Benz awaited their arrival. Magrel and her husband kissed, and he opened the door for her and then for Marcia. On their way home, Sam took them to the mall. "Wow!" exclaimed Marcia; "This is beautiful!" She saw tons of retail shops and escalators. She had never been on an escalator and was afraid to do so. They purchased shoes, clothes, bags, perfumes, slippers, and many more welcome items for her. The final shop before they went home was the cellular store. She had never owned a cellular phone. *Is this really happening?* she thought.

They got home and that was another *WOW*. The house was nothing like the zinc and wooden house she was raised in. To her, this was a mansion. As the car drove into the driveway, two girls ran out shouting delightfully, "They are here!" They opened the car door and descended on Marcia with a barrage of hugs and questions. They joyfully escorted her to her new bedroom. Marcia stood at the door and a wave of emotion overcame her and she began crying. The younger daughter, Simone, ran to get her mother who came in haste. She hugged Marcia and repeated softly to her, "It's ok. It's ok." Magrel assured her that God had favored her, and that she was now in a safe environment.

The room was decorated with a bed covered with a pink and white comforter, two pillows and a bedside rug. There was also a television and a computer desk with a laptop. This caused Marcia to be speechless and she started crying again. Her bedroom had its own bathroom and flushing toilet. Seeing the toilet, her thoughts quickly raised back to the pit toilet she used back home. She also remembered not having real toilet tissue and having to use old newspaper. But things were different now.

She was surprised to find out that her adoptive sisters did not know about the use of clothes lines. The new clothes were washed and dried inside the washing room. She had a draw designated for underwear, one for socks and a dresser littered with perfumes, powder, and cosmetics.

Simone was ten and Susana was one year older than Marcia (16). At dinner, she met her adopted brother, Shawn, but he was not as welcoming as the girls. He was seven years old and refused to acknowledge her. Marcia quickly identified that he was not keen on her being there. After dinner she questioned Magrel privately about his lack of reception. She explained that he is a twin, but his sister died when she was a few months old. He believes she had come to replace his sister. Magrel told her that it would take some time, but that he will come around.

It was bedtime and everyone went to their rooms and closed the doors. Marcia wondered if she should follow their example. Back home, she slept in a passageway with no doors. She did not have her old yard clothes to sleep in nor her night underwear. She was not allowed to sleep in her good panties- those were for school and church only. She was confused but was ashamed to ask anyone for assistance.

She slowly climbed into the bed not wanting to disturb the sheet, and promptly fell asleep in the most comfortable bed that ever existed. She slept and dreamt that she was in heaven, walking with the angels through a beautiful garden. She saw her mother and her grandmother smiling at her and as she ran towards them. But then the sound of Simone calling her woke her. Simone was excited because it was Sunday, and that meant the family was going to church.

CHAPTER

4

Marcia stressed about what she was going to wear to church. They had done all that shopping and neglected to buy church clothes. She took a warm shower and felt like she could stay in the bath forever. She had never enjoyed bathing so much. It was different from using a pale to extract water from the drum at the rear of the house and pouring it into the bath pan. Even the toothbrush was different. This one had an on and off button. When she pressed the on button the brushes rotated.

Uncertain of what to wear, she called Magrel and asked her. She was told to wear a jeans pants, t-shirt, and a sneaker. To Marcia this was blasphemy. Pants to church! Her grandmother would begin speaking in tongues if she heard this madness. Respectfully, Marcia told Magrel that she could never wear pants to church because it is ungodly, unholy and a curse. She continued to explain that females must wear a dress or skirt that falls close to the ankle and their hair must be covered to enter the house of God.

Magrel did not interrupt her during the lecture. Since they got ready early, she took the time to explain to Marcia how the Lord is not so much interested in our outward appearance as much as he is in our hearts. Marcia did not fully embrace the explanations, but it was sufficient to get her dressed in a jeans pant, sneaker, and a t-shirt heading to the sanctuary.

Yet another *WOW*! The church was massive, unlike the wooden structure church she used to attend. This one had inside balconies, projectors a massive choir and children church. It was a mix-racial church, and surprising to her almost everyone had on jeans, shorts, slipper or sneaker. No one was concerned about attire, yet the worship and message preached were incredibly good. Marcia felt at home. She was at peace.

Suzanna introduced Marcia to Mr. Collins, the youth Pastor, and Mr. Warren, the youth choir coordinator. Marcia asked if she could join the choir and Mr. Warren asked her to sing a song. Everyone within earshot was in awe when she began. She had a natural, untainted gift of singing. The youth pastor and a few others drew closer as she sang. She was stopped and given a different song, one with challenging notes. She did it both beautifully and effortlessly. Mr. Warren invited her to rehearsals. It was pointed out that the young lady who was their lead tenor, recently relocated with her parents and they needed that vacancy filled. Marcia was ecstatic. Furthermore, she was informed that the choir had a state tour commencing in two months and everyone must be ready by then. Magrel was overjoyed for Marcia.

The next day Magrel took Marcia to register for high school. "Why are the students not wearing uniforms?" Marcia asked. "What is uniform?" A giggling Simone blurted. Magrel explained the difference in cultures to both girls, and they then exited the car. Marcia noted that the school was like what she had seen in the movies when she had visited Ms. Clarke's home. It was also just like church in that all races of people were present. Students sat on the pavement, grass and on each other's lap. The girls wore makeup, long fingernails and closely fitted clothing. Some even had bright colored hair like, blue and green. The males were handsome. Some played music on their phones and a few were seen trying to hide and smoke.

The principal was friendly, and the registration process was quick and smooth. There was a variety of extra curriculum programs to chose from and Marcia decided on track and field, and robotics. Marcia was now officially a student at the prestigious Malvern Public School. She made a vow to Magrel that she would excel above all her peers. She was determined and believed in excellence in everything she does. She entered in grade ten. The first day of school was challenging. She had difficulty understanding the teachers' and some of the students' accent and vice versa. When she was asked to introduce herself, some of the students laughed when she spoke. Overtime they all learned to understand each other, and Marcia excelled in her classes as she promised her mom.

CHAPTER

5

Church was good. School was good. Home was excellent. However, Mr. Martin was hardly home. He worked as a truck driver and sometimes drove as far as USA. He was gone sometimes for up to three weeks. He always made sure to do video calls and assist with assignments. He was a dedicated Christian father. He accepted Marcia as his own child. She warmed up to him a lot quicker than she expected. Marcia realized that he was a respectful and loving man. She was elated to finally have a father figure in her life.

What is that wailing about, Marcia wondered as she ran towards the sound coming from the living room. Magrel was on the ground with the phone at her ears, weeping. She received a call notifying her that her husband was in a terrible accident and had to be rushed to the hospital. The officer reported that he was delivering goods when two men attempted to rob him. Sam was successful in killing both men but one managed to shoot him in the lower chest. His condition was critical! Suzanna and Simone came into the room. After becoming aware of the current situation they also began to cry uncontrollably. Marcia was tasked with comforting both of them. It was late and Shawn was already asleep. No amount of wailing would wake him up.

The hospital Sam was taken to was a nine hours' drive away. Magrel called the church leaders and requested an immediate prayer vigil. She then called her sister, Andrea, to come stay with the children as she would be flying to see her husband. On her drive to the airport, she remembered how Sam and her had fought about him getting a licensed firearm. He was adamant, but she hated guns. Her father, a former police officer, had accidentally shot himself and was crippled. She consented to him having a gun, but it was not to come into the house. Now she was thanking God that he had it with him.

She prayed the entire journey for his recovery. She said, "God, I cannot raise these children on my own. Marcia needs a father. Please don't take him away from her. We are doing your desire, please don't punish us for obeying you. Lord, I have suffered so many loses, please not another one. Am I the queen of pain? God, I know you are the healing God, and this is not too hard for you. So, I thank you in advance. In JESUS NAME."

She arrived at the airport after a frustrating long two-hour delay at the airport. What greeted her at the hospital was not what she expected. Her husband was nonresponsive and was breathing with the aid of machines. The doctors wrote him off as his chance of recovery was almost zero. Magrel quickly gathered herself together and began to pray. She also contacted her prayer partners and informed them of the situation.

She decided she was not going to eat until her husband became conscious.

She ate or drank nothing for three days and on the fourth day, the doctors saw responses. His fingers and toes moved briefly. Magrel saw hope. She shared the good news with the children and the church. They rejoiced and continued praying.

The incident had an adverse effect on the children. At school, Suzanna got into a fight and Marcia assisted her. They were both punished and sent to the guidance counselor. Simone wet her bed and resented going to school and church. She asked her aunt, "Why would God allow this terrible thing to happen to my dad. Where was God when daddy needed Him?"

Aunt Andrea hugged her, and they cried together.

She was saddened that it took an accident of this nature to be the factor responsible for communication to resume between Magrel and her. They were very close until Magrel found out that her ex-husband and her sister were having an affair. She was devasted and had a nervous breakdown. Magrel divorced Mike and cut off her sister from her life. Andrea was simply happy to be of relevance to Magrel again. She regretted the affair and wished it had never happened in the first place. It all started due to her giving a listening ear to Mike. He was at a low place, and she wanted to give him emotional support. He was not satisfied with his marriage.

He wanted children, but Magrel was unable to conceive and complete a pregnancy cycle. Before Magrel got married to her present husband, she conceived four times for Mike. Unfortunately, all four died as a result of miscarriage. The doctors explained that Magrel had a congenital uterine abnormality, where her uterus was partly divided into two sections by a wall of tissue. This was responsible for the multiple miscarriages.

Andrea's emotional comfort for Mike grew from a listening ear to a sexual entanglement. This went on for three years before Magrel found out. Mike even had the audacity to confess that he and Andrea were trying to have a child. Of course, she didn't actually want a child. Thus, she secretly stayed on contraceptives and blamed the lack of pregnancy on Mike. She told him that his sperm count was low. After Magrel ended the marriage, Andrea continued with Mike for another year because she needed his financial support – she was in her final year of university. Eventually, she ended the affair when her financial situation improved.

It was too much pain and disgrace for Magrel. Her journey to recovery involved professional counseling and much prayer. Mike was her first love, and first sex partner. She thought that he was going to be her one and only. Magrel invested everything, emotionally, spiritually, financially, and mentally into the marriage. "Maybe," she told the counselor in one of their sessions, "if it wasn't my sister, it would be easier to handle. Anyone except my little sister who I took care of after our mother died. This is the worse betrayal ever."

Magrel continued sharing with the counselor. Before the marriage with Mike ended, they had many problems and she often confided in her beloved sister. They cried and prayed together. When she suggested to Andrea that she was going to hire a private investigator because she thought he was cheating, she persuaded her against taking such a low route. She had retorted, "Never allow anyone to pull you to do things outside of your character. Never."

She lamented about the time when Andrea was sick unto death and needed a kidney. Without hesitation she gave her one of hers. At this memory, she began crying. Having lived a life plagued with sorrow and pain, she finally found love and happiness and the person to destroy it was her own flesh and blood.

After several sessions, she forgave Andrea and Mike, but kept them at a distance. Having met Marcia and learned about her mother's demise caused Magrel to return to thinking about her sister. Her present husband who loves her dearly and her beautiful children have never met her. She spoke to her pastor, and he encouraged her to make amends. She decided to invite her to her nephew's birthday party, two months away but the accident happened.

Thank God, Sam made significant improvement and the doctors were convinced that it was a miracle. They had never seen anyone recover from his type of blow. His eyes opened and followed you wherever you went but he was not able to move or speak as yet. Magrel, spent her days in his room praising God. Her desire was to transport him to a hospital closer to their home. She missed her children and her time-off from work was almost all spent.

Sam noticeably improved daily, so the hospital organized an air ambulance to transport him to a recovery trauma hospital close to their home. They arrived safely, but unlike the previous hospital, he had to share a room. His roommate was a man who was severely burn. He was cooking and his gas line had a leak resulting in an explosion. He suffered third degree burns. At first Magrel resisted, but during her prayer session it was clear that she was sent there to minister to that man. The Holy Spirit revealed to her that the man was dying, and he was a backslider (someone who walked away from the faith). She was instructed to do everything she did at the previous hospital. Magrel prayed and worshipped until one day, the man with the burns joined her in singing while crying.

They had a beautiful session in the presence of God and the man recommitted his life to God. He told her his story. His names was Charles Stanley and he had been a youth pastor for many years. After helping so many children stay away and come out of a life with drugs, he himself ended up in that mess. "Be careful if you think you stand, less you fall." He said, His life took a downhill turn. He was out in the dark for seventeen years. Charles lost his wife, children, assets, and friends. Drugs consumed his life. As they prayed, Magrel marveled at the love of God. In honoring his request, she contacted his family and asked them to visit him, but they refused. His eldest son voiced his bitterness, "He's not dead yet? Where is God?" Magrel withheld that information from Charles. The same day Sam spoke, Charles died.

CHAPTER

6

Sam worked for Hanley's Brothers Real Estate and made a small fortune from several investments he pursued. He was raised in the hills of West Virginia to a wealthy family but was excommunicated because he professed Jesus as the Messiah. He had been invited to a college camp meeting and had an awesome encounter with God. His life was changed forever. During the meeting, as the worship team echoed the words of the song, "I am healed, by the spirit of God," miracles began happening. Blind eyes opened, deaf ears popped, and one male and a female jumped out of their wheelchairs. Sam knew at least one of the miracles was certainly not fake. He knew the girl from since they were in middle school. She was injured in a swimming competition and was impaired since. He saw her not only walk but run that evening.

When he was eight years old, he and his brother were playing, and he was accidentally struck in his left eye with a pencil. That left him visually impaired, and he had to wear glasses. That evening, when he saw the miracles and the rejoicing as persons celebrated, he asked God in Jesus name to give him perfect vision. In faith he took off his prescription lenses and has never needed to put them back on again.

He completed college and then acquired his master's degree in theology majoring in missions. It was on his second missionary trip to the Philippines where he met Magrel. He was first attracted to her commitment and love for the work of God. Not long afterwards he saw her beauty. They pursued a long-distance relationship until they got married. He relocated to Canada to be with Magrel.

Sam retired from real estate and started Martin's Trucking Inc. He slowly expanded to having five trucks in his fleet. He manages the administration aspect of the business. The Covid-19 pandemic affected his drivers. One of them lost his life to the virus in 2020. Getting a driver had been challenging and he opted to fill in until he found a replacement. This was challenging for him because it deprived him of family time.

He was big on family bonding. As he lay there after having been shot by the robber, his only prayer was, "Lord, help me to make it back to my family." And yet when he was able to finally speak again the first words that rose from his heart were, "Yes Lord, I am your Missionary." Hearing these words, Magrel wept and rejoiced because she had spoken to him about his absence in ministry. Securing the financial stability of the family had taking precedence and had pulled him away from his calling. She knew he still loved God and His work. Therefore, she prayed that he would find balance.

Sam was his son's hero. He looked up to him. Whenever he was gone trucking, Shawn missed him the most and talked to him as often as possible. They both had walkie talkies and Shawn loved talking on it. Sam vowed to never banish his son, regardless of the choices he might make. One of the most devastating days for Shawn was when his hero failed to be present at his Math Quiz Competition. Sam was unable to make it home in time, due to a snowstorm.

At church, Mr. Martin was the lead minister over the boys' mentorship program. The group had sixty-seven young men from various schools and communities. Most of them were either referred to the group by a counselor, pastor, or the juvenile court. Many of these boys' fathers were absent. Some were dead or imprisoned, and others abandoned their responsibilities. He had a strong support staff who respected his leadership. The boys called him Uncle Sam.

The doctors finally consented to let him go home and finish his recuperating there. Magrel, and the church community planned a beautiful welcome home party. Everyone loved and respected Sam. Some of the boys from the mentorship program were present, as well as members from the police department. After everyone left, he asked his wife about his gun. She told him the police never found it nor the guns of his attackers. When they arrived, all guns were already gone – someone stole them.

Sam put out an ad for drivers with increased salary and benefits and his vacancy was promptly filled. A young immigrant from Nigeria, who had recently relocated with his family, was hired. He was from a Christian background and had many years of truck driving experience. The money from the insurance company was used to expand the company by acquiring another truck. He had always believed that you must be better off after having gone through a crisis. His newly met sister in law's fiancé was grateful for the new driver's position.

He was delighted to meet Andrea and hoped a similar reconciliation could be done with him and his family. He heard about Charles Stanley's passing without being able to meet his family again and was inspired to start praying that he and his aging father would be reconciled. Magrel encouraged him to contact them. He prayed and telephoned his mother. She was super excited to hear his voice. His mom let him know that his father has been waiting for him to call or come home. Mr. Martin Sr. was sixty-nine and was not doing well health wise.

Not long after, the family travelled to West Virginia and their meeting was glorious. Sam's parents finally met their grandchildren and daughter-in-law. They spent three nights with them bonding. Being the first child and only son, Sam's parents asked him to take over the family business. He did not reject the offer, but instead expressed the need to discuss with his wife and pray about it. His father had built a successful poultry industry that supplied meats all over America and Canada.

After much prayer and discussion, he decided not to accept as it would significantly affect his ability to follow through on his promises to God – Missions.

CHAPTER

7

Sam and his parents kept in touch almost daily. His father was still adamant about him taking over the family business. To Sam's surprise, one day his father said, "blessed is him who leaves an inheritance for his children" (Proverbs 13:22). His father became interested in knowing what was so special about Jesus; why his son would willingly walk away from wealth. In his search, he encountered Jesus and surrendered his heart to him.

They made a compromise and opened a head office in Canada where Sam could oversee the entire operation. Sam was keen on the company donating to missions and the boy's mentorship program. Magrel resigned from her job in order to take over the trucking business management for Sam.

Finally, they were in a great financial position with freedom to do missionary outreach. They increased their partnership with Marcia's home church and started a fund in honor of her grandmother. The fund was geared towards helping less fortunate students in Bequia with books, uniforms, and breakfast. The breakfast program became especially popular among the students and their parents.

Marcia committed herself to the choir and did superb on the tour. Mr. Warren was not just a choir coordinator, but a talented songwriter. He was so impressed with Marcia that he spoke to Magrel about Marcia recording a solo. Sam and Magrel spoke to Marcia about it, and seeing her joy and willingness to do it, they gave her their full support. The song was released and became a major hit. Marcia became the new gospel sensation in Toronto. She was interviewed on radio and television. Of course, they asked her about her family and background, but she made sure not to mention any sensitive information regarding her mom or her own sexual assault encounters at the hands of Anthony. Yet somehow someone leaked details of her background. Whoever it was may have done it out of jealousy or bitter strife, but God used it for good. Marcia's story garnered her even more traction among students, inmates and parishioners who could relate with her, or use her story as a source of motivation.

Marcia and Suzan partnered together and recorded a song about the love of God. They sat together with Mr. Warren, and the three of them prayerfully worked on the lyrics while using the holy scriptures as their inspiration. Mr. Warren highlighted that the music they were making was not just about making beautiful sounds, but about worship in Spirit and in truth. The song turned out to be a masterpiece. The girls became known as the singing sisters, as they went around to various church services and events performing the song. They both agreed to give fifteen percent of their earnings to the fund in Marcia's homeland.

Sam and Magrel ensured the girls kept on top of their education. Suzanna, Simone, and Marcia got along quiet well. Although Simone was not as good a singer as her older sisters, their achievements felt like her own success – she was overjoyed for them. There were numerous occasions where the family had to schedule around Suzanna and Marcia, but everyone was fine with it. Everyone except Shawn that is. He felt left out. It seemed like Marcia really had come to steal his family from him. Sam took note of his son's discomfort and called for a family meeting. His main point was that the family should prioritize their quality time together and foster stronger relationships with each other while they had the time.

And time did fly by. In the blink of an eye, Suzanna and Marcia were in college. Since they had cars, they opted to not board on campus. They preferred to commute. Suzanna majored in pharmaceutical and Marcia in Law. Both girls found their first boyfriends and were on top of the world. They did not hide it from their parents. Rather, they made it a family affair. Suzanna and her boyfriend, Marcus, got married immediately after she graduated, but Marcia's relationship ended after seven months. She made a vow to God about sexual purity and her boyfriend resented that vow. He pressured her by claiming she did not love him because she refused to be sexually involved with him. Marcia was hurt by this betrayal. But she wiped her tears and chose to be faithful to her vow. Ever since she escaped that unspeakable situation at fifteen years old, she had vowed to God that she would wait until marriage for sex.

Suzanna relocated to another province but made sure to visit as often as she could. She had two children and continued making songs with Marcia. Marcia remained at home after graduating from law school and assisted her parents with Simone and Shawn. She worked in the family business as one of their lawyers.

Marcia honored her promise to Magrel with regards to academic excellence as evidenced by her graduating at the top of her class. She was even recognized as an ambassador for the university. Marcia remained continually active in the church and became a lay preacher. Eventually she pursued a ministerial license. She loved the word of God and spent much time studying it. Magrel was super proud of her.

CHAPTER

8

Missionary trips can be quite exhaustive. That Wednesday afternoon was certainly that type of a day for Marcia. As she reclined in a hammock, the most handsome man she had ever laid eyes on enquired if she would be interested in having some cold coconut water. Startled, she said no. Then his handsome face glowed. He did not move nor said anything. He simply stood there with the water. She fought the urge to look at him constantly, and that's when she realized the local pastor nodding to her. It seemed as if he was the one who sent the water. She accepted it and the gorgeous man walked away. She immediately threw a barrage of questions at God. "Who is this beautiful man? Is he saved? Is he single? Is he my husband?" It was one of the fastest answers she has ever received from God – Yes, he is your husband.

She called her parents and shared the information. They advised her to continue praying about it and promised to keep her in their prayers. Later that evening, the local Philippine pastor sought her out to let her know that the young man that gave her the water earlier is his son. He went on to share that his son, Michael, fancies her. She also learned that Michael was scheduled to marry three years ago but at the last minute, the bride to be cancelled the wedding.

The next day, she was schedule to return to Canada, but all flights were grounded because of an impending hurricane. Michael took the opportunity to invite her to dinner, which she graciously accepted. During dinner, she asked many questions, and she learned a lot about him. He was disappointed with churchgoers. He grew up in the church all his life and witnessed the hurt and disrespect his father received from the congregants. Although he did not complete high school because of an altercation with a teacher resulting in expulsion, he was presently learning the plumbing trade. However, what he was genuinely interested in was electrical installations. She quickly realized there were no similarities in their future aspirations. She wondered if she heard God correctly – she must continue praying.

The following day Michael drove her to the airport, and they exchanged numbers with the promise to keep in touch. She refrained from telling him what God said to her. At the airport, they hugged, and it was obvious Michael did not want to let go. When he woke up from his daydream he quickly pulled apart. *Wow, he smells and feel good,* Marcia thought and smiled.

Back in Canada, she was excited to share everything with the family including Suzanna who joined in via video call. Marcia returned to work and she and Michael talked every day. Although she had her reservations, she determined to please God.

Therefore, after seven months, they officially decided to date. Both families were excited. After all the pain she has gone through, it was refreshing that God had smiled on her.

Michael and Marcia were asked by their churches to represent them at a major conference in Australia – they joyfully accepted. It was awesome meeting again. They were so excited that they exchanged a spontaneous first kiss. Michael apologized and explained that he does not want to do anything that would be displeasing to God. They instituted some basic ground rules to safeguard their dating from any ungodly interactions. Marcia could not wait to introduce Michael, the perfect gentleman, to her parents and siblings.

Marcia was not about to mess up what God has provided for her. She purposed to make him what she desired. After the conference, she enquired about him furthering his education. She decided, since they are going to be together, she should invest in him improving. They researched schools online and he successfully applied for a college degree from an institution in Ontario. Michael told Marcia that someone had even awarded him a full scholarship. Imagine his surprise when he found out that that someone was Marcia. All she asked of him was to take his studies seriously. They prayed and had a beautiful worship session on the day before he started college. Michael dedicated himself to excelling at college, and with Marcia and Sam's help he was able to get on an accelerated program. This allowed him to finish the program in two and a half years instead of four.

Sam spoke to a friend who decided to hire Michael in Canada. This was much welcomed news as the couple were planning their wedding. Magrel volunteered to be the head planner for their wedding. She remembered that her own mother was not there for her wedding with Sam. She was determined to be there for Marcia.

Michael arrived in Canada and lived in an apartment that her family paid for. His faith in God was renewed and he assisted in the music department of the church. He was an excellent drummer. One day, they went to Niagara Falls and had to overnight. They rented a room at a hotel, and he slept in the chair. He was adamant that they should not share the bed together. This was one of the ground rules they had made very early on in their relationship. He reminded her, "temptation must not be fed." Secretly, Marcia was disappointed. She was expecting at least a kiss and cuddling. But he was not entertaining any of that. Her respect for him increased significantly.

Suzanna, Marcia, and Michael recorded a song about the will of God. Although they got much needed publicity it was not the success they expected. This was all new for Michael. He felt as though his life had new meaning. He loved his fiancé immensely and prayed almost daily that she will not leave like the former girlfriend. He kept dear to his heart what one of the senior apostles told him when they were in Australia – the Lord says, Marcia is your wife.

The wedding was three months away, and they were house hunting. Michael got a new car and enrolled to do his master's degree. They commenced pre-marital counseling, and both discovered that they had wounds that needed healing. Marcia had done well for herself but there were still unresolved issues surrounding the rejection by her mother, abandonment by her father and the death of her grandmother. She discovered that she had not forgiven being rape by Anthony, her neighbor's son. Michael never met his mother, she died in childbirth and his father was physically abusive but taught against abuse from the pulpit. The hypocrisy crushed him beyond his knowledge. He also learned that his ex-fiancé got married to one of his cousins and they were happy together. He was broken. He had trust issues. He believed that people were fake because they hide many truths about themselves. Yet he acknowledged that divulging everything was challenging for him as well. The counselor explained that changes are necessary, painful, and time consuming. They considered postponing the wedding until they were healed but decided against that route.

Michael's greatest fear was disappointing his wife to be. He feared that she will not stay with him. Over the years, everyone he loves either moves away, dies or distances themselves. Thus, as a self-defense mechanism he stopped himself from getting close to anyone for a long time. Another fear he expressed was disappointing his father. His father may have been abusive at times, but he tried to give him the best he could. Michael sincerely hoped he will be able to provide for his father when he is in the winter of his life.

A major difference that surfaced was their dreams pertaining to children. Marcia wanted two, but Michael did not want any. He said that he had witnessed a woman giving birth and he would never put his wife through that horror. He was willing to adopt. Financially, Marcia earned far more than Michael but that was not an issue. At the end of the sessions the counselor advised against pursuing marriage at the moment. He told them that they were not ready to be married as yet; they had differences that needed to be ironed out before tying the knot.

Despite the warning, they were sure that God had brought them together and they were not willing to wait. They found a beautiful house and with the assistance of Sam and Magrel, they purchased it. They agreed on furniture but differed on color scheme for the house. Michael was conservative but Marcia was wild. They compromised and settled in the middle. Sam advised Michael that the wedding was about the wife, so he should let Marcia decide on the decoration. This was challenging for him, but he was humble and teachable.

Michael moved into their house, but Marcia remained with her parents. Her first night there would be after they return from their honeymoon. One day on her way to work she stopped by and Michael was home. He did not hear her enter, as he was praying and crying. Not wanting to interrupt him, she sat quietly and listened to his prayer.

He kept repeating, "How do I tell her, Lord? How do I tell her?" She left without him realizing that she was there. She was troubled and was unable to function at work. She left early and went home to mommy. She was in her room, and Marcia got in her bed and cried. She recounted the morning's occurrences to Magrel, and they prayed asking God to make known to them what was the secret. *Was he gay, dying, or an atheist?* Marcia could only worriedly wonder.

CHAPTER

9

Marcia was super excited, the day that she has dreamed about was finally here. Who would've thought that her dream wedding would approach so quickly? Everything seemed to be coming together just as she planned. The night before the wedding she had a blast. Marcia and her bridesmaids decided to spend a few nights at The Ritz Carlton Reynolds, Lake Oconee in Georgia to unwind before the wedding. Unfortunately for Marcia, sleep never came. A myriad of emotions ranging from joy to anxiety kept her wide awake. Her thoughts were overwhelming! *This day has to be perfect.*

Against the advice of the counselor, the scheduled wedding was here. The bride eventually got some shut eye, but she had to get up at around 7 am. The weather was great – the sun was shining, birds were singing, the air smelled fresh, and there wasn't a cloud in the sky. She went to the bathroom, washed her face, brushed her teeth, and got dressed shortly after. The plan was to meet the ladies for breakfast, but she decided that it was imperative to spend some time alone before things got hectic. *I'll call room service and have breakfast on the balcony,* she thought. She ate quietly and enjoyed the scenery. It was absolutely breathtaking. She was on the 7th floor and could easily see everything beneath. She took in the view – a huge lake that shined like crystals when the sun hit it; an even bigger saltwater swimming pool that was as long as the hotel; huge trees that could provide shade to an entire village; and a wide array of colorful flowers doting the area. Even though she enjoyed how beautiful everything was, what stood out most was the silence. Alone with God and her thoughts, she realized how big the day really was. This was the first day of the rest of her life….Her new life that is.

It was a beautiful sunny Friday morning that 16th of July. All of the invited guests were titivating themselves for the glorious unification ceremony between Michael Rogers and Marcia Rory, slated to commence at 4:30 pm. Magrel had her checklist, and everything was perfect.

Suzanna and Simone were the bridesmaids while Sam, and Shawn were the groomsmen. Grandfather Martin flew over and accepted to be the giveaway father. Michael's father was denied a travelling visa and they were all devastated. Prior to the nuptial, the groom and groomsmen got ready at the matrimonial home and then went to have group pictures taken.

Time flew by quickly and the bridesmaids, photographer, makeup artist and hair stylist came barging into Marcia's presidential suite. Everyone was super exuberant, and she couldn't help but follow suit. The wedding didn't start until 4:30 pm which gave them more than enough time to get ready…. they hoped. Suzanna and Simone got their makeup done first while the stylist worked on Marcia's hair. An hour and thirty minutes passed and finally everyone's hair and makeup were complete. She loved that the makeup artist made sure everyone looked naturally beautiful.

It was now 1:30 pm and the ladies and Marcia decided it was time to start getting dressed for the wedding. But before that they laid out the dresses on the California king sized bed so that the photographer could take a few shots of them. The bridesmaid dresses were a beautiful olive-green color, made from silk fabric with a slight see through mesh attached to the train – very classy.

Her snow-white wedding dress was a gorgeous masterpiece created by one of the top dress designers in Italy; it was modern with a vintage twist. The long see-through sleeves had lace and pearls and the body of the dress featured a mermaid cut that puffed a little at the bottom. It came with an attachable 10-foot train skirt covered in lace and pearl beading that gracefully swept the floor. The back part of the dress was her personal favorite because it had a deep see-through V cut that travels all the way to the bottom of her back and pearl buttons straight down the middle. Her head piece was a splendid blend of diamond and silver and had first been worn by Magrel, and then Suzanna. She was honored to wear it. For a moment Marcia wished her grandmother was present, but she quickly shrugged it off.

Now finally dressed, Marcia was amazed at how breathtaking she looked. Tears filled her eyes, but she fanned them away – she didn't want to ruin her makeup. The photographer snapped a few more photos of them before they headed downstairs to the lobby where a luxurious black Mercedes Benz limo waited for them. Marcia was excited to finally get to the ten-bedroom mansion where the ceremony and reception would be held. They arrived at 2:30pm with time to spare. As they walked through the 11-foot double doors with crystal glass at the front entrance, Marcia could not help but think the place was humongous. It was situated on Ten acres of land.

Michael had serious competition from Grandfather Martin who looked like he was the one getting married. All men were well groomed and smelled exceptionally amazing. Michael was obviously nervous, and they all played their role in setting him at ease. Both Sam and his father told stories of wedding day bliss. Michael video called his father and they all laughed. While getting dressed, Sam gave Michael a few advise on love making and warned him to go easy with his daughter. He told him to not be hasty in penetration as he must ensure she is properly lubricated. Michael blushed and seemed uneasy. Grandfather Martin advised Sam to leave the young man alone – they all laughed, but this sex talk made Michael quite uneasy.

4:30 pm took forever to come. Michael was ready to get this part over with. At 4:00 pm they were all seated. The decorators did an impressive job and persons could be seen capturing memories on their phones. A lady walked up to Michael, stared, and then hugged him. She introduced herself as his mother's first cousin. His father, Pastor Rory, had asked her to represent the family so she flew in from Quebec. She was amazed at how much he looked like his mother. She quickly prayed God's blessings upon him and assured him his mother must be proud of him.

The officiating minister took his place at the podium, and everyone took a seat. The moment they had been waiting for was now. The most melodious sound echoed from an old organ while everyone turned towards the rear, longing to see the bride to be. There was a loud but hidden wow as Marcia graced everyone with her presence. She glided gracefully with Grandfather Martin looking extremely important beside her. Every device that could take pictures became active.

Magrel looked at Sam and tears flowed down her cheeks. She felt a sense of accomplishment. They obeyed the leading of the Lord, and now their hearts celebrate. Since Marcia became their daughter, they cared for her just like their own biological children.

Michael and Marcia wrote their own vows and exchanged them before family, friends and God. She opted to sing a song for Michael, to the cheers of everyone. Her vow ended with the lyrics, "I've got a feeling, that tonight is going to be a good night." Michael blushed and answered, "I pray it is." The documents were signed, and the minister pronounced them husband and wife. Everyone got excited for the kiss and waited eagerly with cameras in hand. The minister began, "You may now…" and Marcia was already smooching Michael. Everyone including the minister laughed. After they finished kissing, the minister completed his statement, "kiss the bride."

The reception had to be cut short and persons got their food to go. The newlywed couple was escorted to the waiting limo and off to the hotel they went. They had a reservation for four nights. Marcia and Michael planned on getting to know each other a lot more intimately.

CHAPTER

10

Marcia smiled as she remembered the last conversation she had with Suzanna. She had handed her a small gift and emphasized that Marcia will need it on the honeymoon. Curious as to what it was, she ensured it was the first gift she unwrapped – it was KY GEL. She was looking forward to using this. Although the newlywed couple were both exhausted, Marcia was sure that they were not going to sleep any time soon. She had kept the promise that she made at fifteen-year-old to walk in sexual purity. It was now time to make love. Marcia was looking forward to a passionate wild time with her husband in a bath filled with water. She hurried to the bathroom and invited her hubby to join her. He came but his steps lacked the excitement she anticipated from him. Almost as if he was dragging his feet.

"This is not true! It cannot be real!" exclaimed Marcia a wife of two hours. The moment she anticipated since the age of 15 years old was finally here, but her water love making fantasy was shattered by her screaming. She ran out of the bathroom, screaming as loud as she could. Wailing, she asked the dreaded question, "Why, God Why?"

She telephoned her mother in a frenzy. Hysterical, she shouted over and over, "Come and get me! Come and get me!" Magrel tried unsuccessfully to calm her down but the phone got disconnected. Magrel woke Sam and shared with him. They purposed not to alarm anyone, and both drove to the hotel the couple was staying.

Marcia came out with all her possessions. Except there was no ring on her finger. They hugged and she wept. They drove home in silence except for Marcia's sobbing. Magrel slept with her that night. Sam did not sleep.

Many questions flooded her mind. *What should I do now? Should I live a lie for the rest of my life, or should I abort the will of God? Was this truly the will of God? Were we deceived by evil spirits? Was this a plot by the ministers to destroy my happiness? Did God really truly love me and if He does why has this evil been given to me? Why, God Why?*

That was a long night for Michael. He knew he should have told her, but he did not know how to. Now his wife whom he loves dearly, ran away. Sitting on the floor, shamed and angry he contemplates suicide. "Why should I continue living?" he asked. He betrayed the person who has shown him love beyond measure. She must be heartbroken. He held Marcia's ring in his hand while he scrolled the internet on ways of committing suicide. He found a site that promises to be your companion through the sacred act of suicide. Viewing the different methods highlighted, he remembered a message his father preached many years ago discouraging suicide. Immediately he closed the browser and started praying. He asked, "Why, God why? Why did you permit this evil upon me?"

Sam telephoned Michael. He needed to know what happened, but Michael declined the call. He knew at that moment; it was prayer time. He walked over to Marcia's room and asked both ladies to join him in prayer. Marcia response was, "No disrespect dad, but I don't want to pray." She followed up with screaming, "Dad, he deceived me, us. He is a liar, a wicked person. I will never trust another man. I should have had sex with him and not wait. It would have been better to repent of fornication, than to suffer this humiliation. According to the law, since the marriage is not consummated, its not binding. I'm out!"

Sam started praying for directives and healing. She interrupted his prayer, "Yes, Michael needs healing. He is the worse man I have ever met. He professes to having a relationship with God, yet his lying lips speaks fluently. Ask God if he was the one who answered my prayer, gave the many confirmations that we are to be together, and please while you are praying, ask God why He would give me a penis-less husband?"

CHAPTER

1 1

"Oh my God, what do you mean penis-less?" Magrel shouted. "That's right mom, my husband, no – Michael has no penis. There is nothing there."

"Does he have a vagina?" Magrel asked confused. "No. Nothing is there, just blankness." Although Sam said nothing, his expression said a lot. Marcia questioned, "Mom, dad, you have been serving God, doing missions, helping the less fortunate, starting churches etc.; Would God give me a penis-less husband? Why would God be so cruel? Tell me, who deccived me; was it God or Michael? I don't know any more if I ever heard God. Does He even speak?"

Michael cried on the phone with his father and asked why? Why would God punish him, and his father has been preaching the gospel all his life? Is God the rewarder of good with evil? Did his condition contribute to his mother's death? Should he stay in the house or get an apartment? What should he say to his wife, Magrel and Sam? He decided to leave Canada. Leave the mess he made.

Michael confided to his father that he would be leaving Canada, but he had no intention of coming home. He is going to a different country to get a new start. He told him, he will get in touch as soon as he settles. Against his father's wish, Michael disconnected the call. Michal's father telephoned Sam and apologized for his son's condition and him not telling Marcia. He also shared that he was concerned for Michael's safety. Sam attempted to leave to check on Michael, but Marcia got so mad that he refrained. She was upset that he was about to leave his daughter to seek out a deceiver.

Later that day, Sam went to the should be matrimonial home, but Michael was not there. On the kitchen table, he found a note which started with an apology but ended with, 'see you in the next life' – a suicide note. Frantically, he called Magrel and 911. Michael must be found and stopped. He searched the house but nothing. He telephoned Michael's father and informed him about the situation. Pastor Rory suggested he check under the bed. As a child Michael had a habit of hiding under the bed when he was challenged with stressful situations.

Sam found him under the bed, foaming and frothing from the mouth. He had overdosed with over-the-counter painkillers. He was dying. The emergency response ambulance and fire rescue vehicles arrived a minute apart from each other. They raced into the house and immediately attended to the nonresponsive Michael. He was rushed to the North York General Hospital where he was admitted in critical condition. The church was notified, and persons began to pray.

Marcia was very hot in unforgiveness and bitterness and responded in like manner. She did not empathize and continued watching a documentary on the animal kingdom. Magrel, raced out of the house and sped to the hospital. She and Sam united in prayers. Suzanna arrived at the house to be with Marcia and the two sisters cried and cried.

Marcia asked Suzanna if they could get away for a few days. She wished to visit Aruba to clear her head. Suzanna discussed it with her husband, who consented, and the girls were off. Suzanna believed that she needed to be there for her sister. They arrived safely and checked in at the beautiful Brickell Bay Beach Club Boutique Hotel & Spa. Magrel warned Suzanna not to initiate any conversation about Michael. She struggled to not bring it up but she complied.

The second night while drinking a glass of margarita wine, Marcia confided to Suzanna that she no longer believed in God. She could not believe a loving God would allow her to be deceived nor deceive her. She planned to resign from all her portfolio at church, and no longer sing any more gospel music. Suzanna was astonished but allowed her to speak. Marcia claimed it was unfair for God to punish her for the wrongs of her mother and that that kind of unforgiving God, cannot and would not get her worship. She also shared her plans of moving into the matrimonial home by herself. If Michael survived, he would not have any access to it. She sincerely hoped he didn't live.

Fortunately, Michael was resuscitated and stabilized. He remained unconscious and Sam stayed with him. After 4 days he was released with orders to get counseling. He rented an apartment and stayed away from church. He believed everyone knew about his condition and he just wanted to disappear. He commenced counseling and was happy he did. The counselor informed him about a man from Manchester England, Robin Johnson, who had received treatment for a similar condition. The counselor told him that he would send him a

YouTube link to a video on Johnson's story, but Michael was so excited he asked if they could watch it together right there and then. At the end of the video Michael was relieved that not all hope was lost.

CHAPTER

1 2

Marcia went back to work and pretended everything was fine. However, she secretly started sessions with a counselor. A few weeks into what should have been her honeymoon vacation, she met David at a bar that lawyers usually frequent. He was a handsome, well-spoken attorney. They went on a few dates. He was charming and had a bright future in the firm he worked. But he was an atheist. At first, this was -a concern, but then she saw it as a good thing, because she too was now a professing atheist.

One Friday evening, they went to a after work party hosted by one of his friends. By the time they were ready to leave they were both drunk. Despite being well aware of the possible legal and medical dangers involved of driving under the influence, they still decided to drive themselves home. They got lost. David pointed out a homeless man and suggested to Marcia that they ask him for directions. The man was also drunk but managed to give them proper directions. Marcia handed him some monies and the man refused it. In turn he offered her these words, "If you know what is good for you, you quickly return to God." Those words pumped the intoxication out and she became sober immediately.

Yet, she resisted. She fought to suppress acknowledging the miracle that happened. She got to her house and invited David in – she wanted sex. Upon entering her house, David was surprised at the beauty and warmth. He noted that it feels like a cozy matrimonial home. She kept that a secret. She pounced on him, and just as she was about to kiss him, he stopped her. He enquired about what the drunk man had whispered to her earlier.

She asked him to forget that and just enjoy the ride. She desperately wanted to have sex. Just when she started wondering why David was acting so strange, he acted even weirder. His facial expression changed drastically as if he had just seen a ghost. Petrified, he stammered, "Who, who, who are you? What have I, I, I done to you to de, de, deserve this? Pl-, ple-, plea-, please don't let them kill me" She was startled by the words that proceeded from his mouth. Her facial expression told him that she was unaware of what he spoke about. David, still shaking, pointed to two men with swords who were looking angrily at him. Marcia looked but failed to see what he described. She then realized that he was seeing angels.

David addressed the angels and begged for his life. He threw the blame on Marcia saying that she was the one who invited him. As David begged, he said one of the men told him to confess his hidden secret to her or he shall die. With tears flowing down his face, he revealed his secret – he was HIV positive. Her knees became weak, and she collapsed to the ground.

Without delay she cried out asking God for forgiveness. She also prayed that God may have mercy on David.

David relayed to her that one of the men said she must ask for healing for him, and that Michael is her husband. At those words, she wailed. After a good cry, she prayed for David's healing from HIV. Marcia explained to David that she was a Christian but backslid and that Michael was indeed her husband. She further testified that God is real and the men he saw were angels. So, David asked what must he do to be saved? She led him in the sinners' prayers, and he accepted the Lord Jesus as his savior. Before the angels left, they told David that he was healed.

CHAPTER

1 3

Magrel called Marcia, informing her there was someone at the house to meet her. Upon arrival, she saw a white well-groomed gentleman who looked to be in his late sixties. He was smiling at her. He introduced himself as Dave Alexander, her mother's ex-husband. He stumbled upon an article where she was interviewed by the local newspaper. When he saw the name Ruth Dailiah Watson, he knew it was his ex-wife. Marcia was stunned and could hardly contain herself. Dave said he was on vacation and thought of meeting her. They exchanged numbers, promised to stay in touch and spent the afternoon talking, until it was time for him to leave.

After Dave left, Marcia called everyone together and connected Suzanna on the phone line. She shared her encounter with David, the drunken man, and the angels. She then asked the dreaded question again, "Why God why?" She was still lost as to why God had given her Michael as her husband. She told them that before the angels left, they confirmed that Michael is her husband.

Unsure of what type of reception she would receive, she went to see Michael at work. He was stunned to see her, his heart raced a bit faster, and he wondered why she was there. Reluctantly, he approached her cautiously. She smiled and proceeded to apologize for the way she handled the situation. She sincerely asked for his forgiveness. Likewise, he apologized for not being transparent and asked her for forgiveness. She recounted everything that took place and asked that they start afresh. He danced in jubilation, praising God for answering his prayers.

That night Marcia came to God in prayer. She was honest with God as she cast her cares on Him, "God I don't know how to proceed, what to do, where to turn but I will trust you. I surrender my future to you. My marriage, my life is in your full control. I submit to your wisdom. In Jesus name, amen."

Michael moved back into the matrimonial home. Although penal penetration was not available, they were very intimate with each other. He was a true gentleman. He opened the doors, held her hand while they walked, ensured her cell phone was charged before she left out of the house in the mornings and her lunch was packed. She loved to cuddle and kiss and he ensured she was not lacking. He substituted his penal functions with all available body parts that were useable. She enjoyed their intimacy… but the absent member was missed.

They discussed sex aid and agreed on getting a dildo. Marcia agreed to the condition that it only be used when both of them are together. They made a big deal out of getting this dildo and decided to shop online. After a painful and frustrating one hour, they agreed on size and color. The newest member to the family arrived and was activated as soon as it was out of the package. Marcia fell in love with it whereas Michael became depressed. Although he was the inserter, he wanted to be the direct agent pleasuring his wife. He resented the new member. As he penetrated his wife, he remembered the YouTube video he watched on Robin Johnson.

After they showered, he shared with her about Johnson's surgical treatment. He informed her that there are other options presently available. She was excited and asked why he took so long to share. He said he was afraid to be disappointed. They watched the videos and decided to research further.

They researched the surgeons who operated on Johnson, and they recommended a doctor in Canada. Although the procedure cost a lot of money, they decided on proceeding. The surgeries if successful, would grant Michael a functional bionic penis.

The first meeting with Dr. Ismalik was terrifying – they didn't know what to expect. He reassured them that it is possible. He was confident as he had done this procedure before although Michael's condition is a rear occurrence. Marcia sighed internally when she found out it only affected one in every five million males. Dr. Ismalik made it clear that it would take a series of operations, five to be exact. Surgeries were successful and after two months of the final one, Michael received the green light to engage in sexual activities.

They were both excited. It was time to celebrate. Marcia could be heard singing the lyrics, "tonight is going to be a good night" throughout the day. They went out to a beautiful restaurant and had a delicious dinner with fine wine. They got home and had a worship session, thanking God for his favour over their lives.

Michael did a lot of research online and he was excited to try out his newly developed art. He was ecstatic to not need the dildo and secretly threw it out. They kissed, caressed but Marcia was eager to go from foreplay to penetration. She whispered sweetly in his ear, "please enter me…" The erected Michael obliged and cautiously penetrated his wife for the first time with his own penis.

Marcia was on top of the world as she straddled her husband. She was about to climax when Michael let out a wretched scream in agony. "Oh no," Marcia exclaimed, "Why God Why?"

PART 2

CHAPTER

1 4

"Is he crazy?" screamed Marcia, as the ambulance driver narrowly escaped an accident with a vehicle that refused to stop at an intercession. Before that outburst, "Oh God, please, please" were the only words heard from her. She was torn between fright for Michael's health and their safety. Nee nor! Nee nor! blared the racing siren. Was it the speed of sound or light, she couldn't tell, but she was certain no ambulance should go this fast. Nevertheless, she wondered, *are we soon there?*

Jesus, Jesus! I have always thought ambulances were more noise than speed. Is this driver aware that I'm driving behind him? Marcia desperately tried to keep pace with the flying ambulance.

Red, white, red, white, seemed to be all she saw as the ambulance's lights kept flashing. This was the first time she had driven with her hazard lights blaring. The only time they eased acceleration was approaching and passing a stop light on red. The intense focus required from her, robbed her of noticing the eyes of pedestrians and the curious looks on the face of motorists who yielded to the demand of the blazing siren.

"What's happening, why is he stopping?" Marcia asked to no one in particular. She stopped her car and ran towards the ambulance, asking, "What's wrong, what's wrong?" "Are you kidding!" she exploded to the EMT's reply of engine failure. *Why, God Why?*

The driver realized that something was wrong from the onset of their trip back to the hospital. Thus, he was desperately trying to make it to the hospital. By the time the engine failed, they were four minutes out and a replacement ambulance had already been dispatched. It took less than a minute for the replacement to arrive and mere seconds to transfer the patient from one vehicle to the other. *Thank God,* Marcia sighed as they were in motion again. Marcia was not sure whether the second driver was briefed on the urgency of the situation or just had a 'this patient will not die on my watch' mentality. However, what was certain is that his reckless speed matched that of the first driver.

They rushed Michael into surgery, where Dr Ismalik and a team of doctors were on standby. "He's, my husband!" Marcia shouted as a burly security barred her from going into the surgical room. "Sorry, it's nothing personal. Just enforcing hospital protocol," replied the calm security guard who was no stranger to disgruntled family members.

At that moment, she realized she had not locked the doors of her car. She ran outside to park and secured the car properly. On her return, all she could do was intense waiting. Something felt strange. Something was off. What was it? A nurse approached her and politely offered her a pair of slippers. Marcia smiled at the realization that she was barefoot all along. She thanked the nurse and received her gift with gladness.

Marcia hates waiting. She thought waiting at the airport was the worst it could get. You could wait at the airport all day, just to hear that your flight was cancelled, and you would have to come back the next day to continue waiting. But this wait at the hospital was monstrous. There is no coming back another day if your loved one dies. No one came with any updates. She felt as though she was sitting in utter darkness waiting to hear God say, "let there be light." A rush of hospital personnel disrupted her thoughts as they raced outside to meet three newly arrived ambulances. This was followed by the pushing of beds, persons crying in pain, and doctors and nurses shouting instructions. The quiet hospital suddenly plunged into a scene of chaos. Marcia overheard that a bus carrying tourists had a head-on collision with a trailer. A strong police presence was evident, and she wondered who criminal charges will be brought against.

Her grumbling stomach set her in search of the cafeteria. She ordered a medium bowl of red peas soup and a bottle of water. The food looked and smelled inviting. Unfortunately, her concern for her husband drowned her appetite. She settled for a small sip of water, covered the food, and began praying. *Lord, you are the great healer, I ask you in the name of Jesus to recover my husband. Amen.* She walked back to the waiting area and made herself comfortable.

"Mrs. Rory, Mrs. Rory," accompanied by gentle patting on her hand pulled her out of a dream that she was enjoying. It was Dr. Ismalik. Once she was alert enough, he informed her, "Your husband is out of surgery and will be able to see you in an hour. He will be ok but will be retained in the hospital for three nights of observation." A hospital worker joined them and had her signed a few documents, while Dr.

Ismalik continued speaking, "We have a concern which we can discuss with you afterwards. It's nothing serious, just an observation."

"Dr. Ismalik," she interrupted, "I remember categorically enquiring if there were anything that we should be concerned about, and you said no. Yet we are here today, with Michael in recovery and I'm here confused." Dr Ismalik did not address her rattling, but rather requested, "please tell me what happened." He sat beside her.

CHAPTER

1 5

"Michael, I don't think we have an appointment today – did I mess up my schedule again? Please forgive my manners, good morning." A confused looking Michael tried to respond but words were distant from his expressions. Joy (Michael's counselor) pointed to a sofa, asking him to be seated. She closed the door and enquired what was the meaning of this ad hoc visit.

With his cheeks caressed by tears, he managed to say in a soft controlled tone, "Why God Why?" Joy remained silent and gave him time to speak without interruption. After a two minutes pause, Michael still crying pondered out loud, "Who am I? Am I cursed? Will anything good ever happen for me or has God closed his eyes and ears to my pain? I have suffered beyond the capacity of ten men. I have escaped my breaking point, but now it has captured my mind, body and soul. I cannot! I cannot do this any longer. The psychological mountain of failure is too high and wide for me to pass – I am tormented. Have you ever been lost in darkness and miraculously you see a light? Your hopes that were dead, suddenly are restored. But when you pick up the pace and arrive at the light, your efforts were in vain! Why? Has the struggling candle breathed its last breath and died?"

Joy shifted her body posture and leaned towards Michael and softly said, continue. However, he paused, seemingly unable to get any more words out. Not wanting him to shut down as he had done in the past, she suggested a session of the empty chair. Once he agreed, she asked, "Who would he like to address?" His response – everyone. They decided to allot ten minutes per person. The room was rearranged to facilitate the new direction of the session, and Michael's body language explained he had done this before.

He unleashed a fury of questions first to his mother. "I have heard three varying accounts as to your death, which is true? Is it true that you abandoned me because my father cheated on you with the secretary of the church and it threw you into depression which you never recovered from? Is my father responsible for me being born without a penis? Did he stress you to the point of me not developing completely? Did you die from an overdose of drugs? How could you be pregnant and doing drugs? Did you not care for me? And finally, is it a family curse?"

Michael's mother, Antoinette, was the third of four girls for her mother. All four girls had children but no sons. The only exception was Antoinette's baby boy, Michael. This has always puzzled Michael. A rumour that was hushed, says, his grandfather was drunk one evening and raped a lady from a neighboring community. Allegedly, a curse was pronounced against him so that no sons shall come from his loins. "If the curse was true, am I a female living in a male's body?" Michael said in anguish. At that utterance, he looked at Joy with piercing eyes, which caused her to shiver internally for two seconds. She saw a Michael that was different. She saw the true struggle.

He stormed out of the office but returned after three minutes. He sat down quietly, as though nothing happened. Joy was confused. She had never seen him act in this manner before. She offered him a bottle of water – he rejected it. Michael declared in a stern voice, "I am a man. I am not confused as to who I am. My name is Michael Rory and that's final."

Looking at Joy, Michael posed a question she was not prepared for, "Is God fair?" He had been asking himself this question for a while now. Why would God allow this evil to be his portion when his father has been serving Him faithfully? Why would God curse him and not overturn it and he has been serving Him for the past 15 years? Why does it seem like Christians are cursed and heathens are blessed?

After a minute of silence, Michael added, "There is a concealed recurring thought that plagues me occasionally – am I a dislocated female?" Joy remained silent and allowed him to think, breathe and resume speaking. He continued, "I love my wife, she is a gem. God showed me His love for me by gifting me with her. Did you know I threw out the dildo? It made her so happy that I was jealous. Oh, foolish I was! How could I destroy what gave her pleasure?" In tears, Michael got up and walked out of the office. This time it did not look like he was coming back.

Joy thought it unwise to allow him to leave in the state he was in, so she ran after him. "Michael,

Michael." she called, but he ignored her plea for him to stop. She caught up with him and asked him to return to the office. He cursed her bitterly. He blamed her for all this additional pain he incurred. Joy introduced hope to him, and it only brought him sorrow, pain, and expensive medical bills. She apologized for his disappointments but reassured him that all hope is not lost.

Michael left the counselling session in such a low mood that he cancelled the date he had planned with Marcia. Instead, he opted to have a drink at a secluded bar and restaurant. On his third drink, three men entered the bar, and pursued robbing the patrons. As they disarmed every one of their valuables, one patron pulled his firearm from off its ankle holster and fired hitting two of the criminals – one died. The third one escaped but managed to shoot the hero patron before leaving. While lying on the ground as though dead, Michael reflected on how his selfishness caused him to be in this mess. He could have been dinning with his beautiful wife, but there he was laying on the ground with shots being fired.

The shots ceased and the atmosphere was then saturated with voices. Some rejoicing, one wailing and others shouting, "don't let him die!" What was a few minutes earlier, a quiet chill spot for persons who wanted to just hide away, was now the scene of death, blood, and chaos. Rising from the floor slowly, Michael saw for the first time a dead body in real life. He was shaken, yet thankful. The patron who challenged the robbers, revealed that he was a businessman whose finances were experiencing a drought and he just wanted a quiet place to process life.

The ambulance and police arrived and attended to the wounded men – criminal and businessman. Both were rushed away in ambulances. Then suddenly, a loud outburst of "Don't kill me!" rose above the noises that were still present at the crime scene. The escaped robber, slowed down by his gunshot wound, did not make it very far. Two police officers combing the area, followed a trail of blood with guns in hands. They found him hiding under a jeep in the parking lot.

To the officer's surprise, the would-be robber was a police officer. One was overheard telling him that he had disgraced the force and he deserves to die. The other one was more sympathetic because he knew the young officer's plight. His only child, a two-year-old son who lives with his mother in Jamaica, was in dire need of a costly surgery. He applied for loans but was promptly rejected due to a lack of financial history in Canada as a recent migrant. Michael overheard the poor cop's story and decided to give the sympathetic officer his contact number indicating that he would love to help the child.

Michael called Marcia and told her all that happened. She was scared but thankful that he was ok. He informed her about the child and they both decided to help. Their conversation was interrupted by a police officer who was documenting evidence. She asked

Michael to tell her what happened. With Marcia online, he recounted all he could remember.

CHAPTER 16

"Michael." a calm Marcia said as she beckoned to her husband to sit beside her. Without any verbal response, a distraught looking Michael complied. She continued, "Since we got married, it's like we have been hit by a speeding train and thrown into a river of strong current. We have not gotten a break. We must pool together and find the solution from the Lord. You are the priest of this house; I need to hear from you. How can I submit to what I am unaware of? My husband, I know things are not as how we would love, but in pleasing God, we must let our marriage work. I am not upset, annoyed yes but not angry. Your facial expression says you have no idea what I am talking about. I have accepted that I will not produce children from my womb; I will never experience pregnancy. But should I accept not being able to find in our home, what belongs to me? Where is my dildo?"

Embarrassed, Michael sidestepped the question and said, "This morning I went to the counselor – unscheduled, cancelled a date with you, and went to a bar, got robbed, experienced gunshots being fired in my vicinity, saw blood, and a dead body. I would appreciate, a hug, 'thank God you are safe, I was worried' or 'tell me what happened.' Instead, you have changed your apparels from concern wife to loss and found investigator. Can you get any more insensitive? When did it become your dildo? We bought it together and agreed that it must only be used when we are together. That's the reason I threw it out. I knew you…"

Marcia interrupted his rattling's with, "You did what?" Her voice pitch increased rapidly as she transitioned from annoyed to irate. Mr. Rory, do you hate me so much that, the one pleasure you have been able to give me since we got married, you took away. I hate you; I super hate you! I have submitted to your short coming and how have you repaid me? I need a divorce today!"

Michael got up and slowly walked over to his wife and hugged her. As his hands held her, she faintly tried to escape his loving arms. With words between tears, she confessed, "I love you. I love God and I want to be happy. I want us to be happy." Sobbing she continued, "I know you have challenges, and you feel insufficient, but I am here for you. Let us unite and grow together."

Michael sat down and received her onto his lap. He stared at her and apologized for her pain. He explained that he threw out the dildo because he had become jealous of the love she showered on the dildo; He felt that he was competing with the dildo to pleasure her. She laughed and told him he was crazy. They kissed and embraced each other. She laughed and told him half-joking, half-serious, "You are buying back my dildo…sorry our dildo." After showering, they both ate and ended up shopping online for the replacement.

Marcia's excitement was short lived when their replacement package arrived. It was the same color but was slightly smaller than the original. She was not about to settle. Michael examined it but refrained from commenting. Marcia repackaged and proceeded to return to sender. She was more than willing to wait a few more days for a satisfactory product.

The following day, they decided to commute together in an effort to spend more time together. As they drove, Michael held her hand and uncertainly asked, "What about adoption?" As though she anticipated the topic, Marcia quickly responded, "Boy or girl?" He said, "Both," and laughed. On that note, Marcia asked if he heard anything from the police officer regarding the child in Jamaica. He said no but promised to follow up.

Not long after, Marcia and Michael confirmed that they were going on the mission field – heading to Jamaica. It was prophesied to them that they were called to be missionaries, and here they were. Shawn, Marcia's adopted brother heard about the trip and was pleased to come along. This was his first flight to the Caribbean, and he planned on enjoying every moment. He had even collated a list of must visit places - Dunn's River Falls, Port Royal, Bob Marley Museum, just to name a few.

Marcia did not enjoy air travel. In contrast, Shawn was so excited that the four-hour flight seemed short. He was not shy in broadcasting his exhilaration, especially after one of the air hostesses bumped him up to first class from economy. All throughout the flight his cellphone received no rest – Tik Tok and Instagram were constantly lit up. Once they landed, they were able to clear immigration and customs relatively easily. They were soon drinking cold local coconut jelly water from a vendor outside the airport.

They collected their rental car and headed to the Bustamante Children Hospital where baby Romain was admitted. The hospital staff was informed of the missionaries visit and the administration staff ensured a warm reception. "What's the matter?" Marcia asked, as she observed the changed facial expression of the nurse doing the temperature check. Michael and Marcia's temperature were elevated. Consequently, they had to be separated and tested for Covid. They were both positive. All three of them had to be quarantined.

"This can't be happening!" exclaimed Shawn, "I refuse to waste my vacation locked up in a hotel room." Meanwhile, Marcia and Michael transferred the surgery fees to the hospital to much delight. The hospital facilitated them seeing the baby via video call. He was super tiny and was crying throughout the call. His mother tried to speak to them but was too emotional. She was aware that her husband had tried to rob Michael, so it was hard to comprehend how he would turn around and help their baby. She sent an appreciation gift of a handcrafted wooden map of Jamaica. Marcia and Michael loved it. "Where is Shawn? He is not in his room." asked Michael. "I thought he was there." Marcia quipped. "I can't believe this child decided to violate his quarantine."

CHAPTER

17

"I was previously engaged to be married and hours before the wedding date she canceled." Michael confessed to his wife. Truth is when he first saw his ex-fiancé, he was not interested in her, but rather her friend. However, Janet, his ex, looked like she was in need and wanted a friend, so he engaged her in a conversation. Their friendship blossomed quickly, and in no time, Michael considered her his best friend. They dated for a while until he confessed to her about his shortcoming; He trusted her enough to tell her that he did not have any penis. Yet she appeared to remain resolute in her love for him. He asked her to marry him, and she excitedly agreed. But on the wedding day, she was a no show. About four months later she got married to his cousin. Michael had heard the rumors that she was cheating on him, but he never believed it until that betrayal.

He was devastated. But she was not done hurting him. While they were dating, they agreed that they would never expose each other's secrets if they broke up. However, Janet, did not hesitate to expose his condition. He was so humiliated; the entire world knew that he was without penis. It was challenging for him to come out of the house. Thus, he isolated himself for almost a year. He was angry, bitter. He fantasized about killing her, but he knew that he could not go through with it himself. Someone told him about a hitman. He made contact and even paid the deposit. He wanted her dead. Darkness engulfed him and he made his home in the pitch-black coldness. He declared that there will be no peace for him until she is buried.

The church his father pastors had a 21 day fast and on the 8th day, his father called him. He delivered the Lord's message, " Son, the Lord said you are planning evil, but you must refrain and trust Him." As his father continued, he mentioned how God warned Cain before he killed Abel. Michael tried desperately to contain the tears, but he became broken before his dad. His father prophesied, "God says that which has left your life, was not the best He had for you, and He will be sending your soul mate to you. God said, you will be victorious after much pain. There is pain in the will of God."

Michael stared at Marcia intently in the eyes and told her, "I feel stuck, as if he I am not making any progress. It seems the more I advance, the more I get pushed down. I am tired, very tired." Marcia held his hand and gave it a comforting squeeze. He reverted to explaining what happened. He said he canceled the hit, but he was still being threatened to pay the balance. He did not have direct contact with the hitman, but the middleman was pressuring Michael to pay up. Michael did not have the monies and he was terrified. He went into repentance and fasting about it until the person stopped contacting him.

After he committed his life to God, one day in prayer, the Lord directed him to take some monies to his runaway bride to be. He was stunned and replied by rebuking the devil. He opened his bible and Romans 12:14, 'Bless those who persecute you, bless and do not curse,' popped out at him on the first page he turned to. He also received word of knowledge concerning the matter – his ex was sick and lacked the financial resources required to get proper medical attention. God spoke yet again with more firm specific commands to help her.

Reluctantly, Michael obeyed, and she was shocked to see him. Janet was embarrassed to take the monies and apologized for breaking their covenant. She confided in him that she got pregnant for a coworker and concocted a home remedy to induce an abortion. Although she terminated the pregnancy, not all of the contents of her womb passed through. Hence, she needed monies to be attended to by a private medical facility. Janet confessed that she had cheated on Michael with her present husband while they were still together. She begged for his forgiveness. He was finally able to truly forgive her. Michael gave her the money, prayed with her, and then left.

When he was out of her eyesight, he sat on a stone under the shade of a mango tree. He wept tears of joy. Strangers passing by could see him doing his happy dance. He rejoiced even more as he remembered what the Lord told him through his father. Everything made perfect sense. Janet was definitely not a good match for him; It was a blessing that their relationship had not worked out. His faith and confidence were drastically strengthened. Michael said that he was trusting God to send him his soul mate.

As Marcia listened to her husband, she felt compelled to share her own story. She started, "When I was 14 years old, a friend, Natalie, and I experimented in being girlfriends…" She explained how they hid their relationship until her friend's mother eventually found out. The mom took them to a spiritualist man for him to cleanse them of the spirit of lesbianism. The man said he had been getting quite a few cases like this and he had successfully rid them of the evil spirit. The remedy of course had a monetary price tag. Before he could administer the cure, he had Natalie's mom sign a contract, which Marcia later recognized to be a consent form for him to have sex with them; the cure was sex. The monies were paid, and he took them into a bedroom one by one. He tried to be gentle, but he was big. He gave her an experience she had never had before nor after – an orgasm.

After the girls left, they abstained from each other. Natalie was not cured and was just keeping her distance from Marcia in an effort to convince her mom that she was no longer same-sex attracted. However, after a while she found another girlfriend and moved out of her mother's house. The mother-daughter relationship was strained, and they were never able to reconcile as Natalie's mom died. Natalie grieved the loss of her mom and wished that her mom had accepted her.

On the other hand, Marcia loved the high she got from the spiritualist. She went back to see him, pretending to have left something there. He told her; he had been waiting on her to return. They had a sexual relationship for about 6 months. It ended abruptly when one Sunday at church a praying mother discerned everything she had been doing through the Spirit. The lady hugged her and prayed for her. During the prayer, Marcia was moved to tears and vomited a lot. The prayer was very private although they were in the congregation; no one else knew her secrets. She never visited the spiritualist again.

CHAPTER

18

"Shawn, where were you? What happened?" A concerned Marcia asked. Shawn replied, "I had a blast! I met a beautiful lady who was fascinated with my accent, and she volunteered to be my escort. I went to Port Royal, its beautiful. We had fried fish and festival, walked the giddy house, and learned about the earthquake of 1692. The only problem is all the monies I had… is finished." 'What!" exclaimed Marcia, "What do you mean finished?" Shawn explained, "We are going out tonight and she needed clothes for herself and her two sisters. So, we went shopping. It was a bit challenging for me to figure out the conversion of monies, so she helped me with it. Her sisters were also awesome, and…" Shawn was interrupted by Marcia and Michael's laughter. "Shawn, my brother, you have been swindled. Do you have a contact number or address for these beauties?" Shawn got a little defensive, "Yes, I do." Michael chimed in, "Ok, please call one of them." "She has my phone. My number is international so she took my phone so I could easily contact her from either of your phones." Shawn's statement was met with further laughter. The expression on his face was one of complete loss.

Out of humor, Marcia, dialed his number but surprisingly to Shawn it did not even ring – it went to voice note. Reality finally hit Shawn with a force that sent him sitting on the ground – he was bamboozled. How could he have fallen for their tricks. Shawn started thinking out loud from the shock, "the kiss and our time at the guess house…was that a lie too?" "What do you mean time at the guest house?' questioned a no longer laughing Marcia, "Did you have sex with those girls and if you did, did you use a condom?" "Yes, and yes," muttered Shawn. "That was my first sexual encounter. And it was all a lie. I'm done, I'm ready to go."

Marcia wanted to simultaneously scold and comfort her little brother. But then her phone rang. "Hello, dad." Marcia answered. "Is everything ok? We have been trying to get a hold of Shawn, but his number doesn't ring." "Dad, please don't be upset, Shawn gave away his phone and all the money he had. He found love and love found his pocket and phone." Magrel was overheard saying, "What do you mean? Is he ok? Let me speak with him."

Their quarantine time ended, and they extended their trip by three days. The beauty of Port Royal that Shawn spoke of, excited the couple so they all went there. While eating, Shawn suddenly shouted,

"Mitsie, Mitsie!" to a young lady that was eating with an elderly gentleman. She completely ignored him. Shawn explained that she is the girl he had sex with and bought clothes for. In fact, he bought the blouse she was wearing, and she had his phone. Michael advised him to let it go, but he refused. Shawn said, "that phone was my 16th birthday present, and I want it back."

Shawn went over and confronted the young lady, who looked disturbed at his accusations. "Do I know you?" She asked. "Yes, Mitsie, I bought you the blouse you are wearing and that phone you are using is mine." He spoke while trying to contain his anger. Still pretending, she responded, "Firstly, I don't know you and my name is not Mitsie." The elderly man politely asked Shawn to please excuse himself and cease creating a scene. Michael and Marcia went and got Shawn, but before he walked away, he told the gentleman, "Sir, please look at the rear of her phone, you will see an s engrafted. Both the girl and the man laughed and told him to go with his family."

Marcia comforted Shawn and promised to replace the phone if it was not on insurance and Michael gave him some money. Their next stop was the Bob Marley Museum followed by a trip to Devon House. Marcia had heard that Devon House boasts to have the best ice cream on the island. Although tired, they decided on one more stop – Emancipation Park. It was beautiful and relaxing. There were several persons walking around for exercise and some couples relaxing on benches. On their way back to the hotel, they drove through New Kingston and Shawn shouted, "Is that Mitsie?" Michael turned around the car and passed by a few ladies on the street. A quick glance easily revealed they were prostitutes vying for customers, and yes, Mitsie was there.

As though seeing her on the street brought healing to Shawn, he started laughing. He muttered the words, "She got me." But he was not satisfied. He actually wanted to help her. "Michael," Shawn said, "can we help her to get out of prostitution? We are missionaries, and this sounds like an assignment." So as to not discourage his bravery while not supporting his cause, Michael responded thus, "If we see her tomorrow, we will take it as a sign." That night Michael prayed that they would not see Mitsie again.

Shawn tried extensively to wash away Mitsie from his body and memory. He lost sleep over this. He was awake by 3:45 am riddled with questions. Why was Mitsie selling her body? Where are her parents? Does she goes to school? How old was she? Later that morning, they drove to Dunn's River Falls, and it was more fantastic than they expected. Again, his Instagram and Tik Tok were on fire. But although he was having fun, the time seemed to drag by slowly. His mind was on Mitsie.

They got back to the hotel exhausted. After they had a hearty lunch, Shawn advocated for them to go to New Kingston to prove that God still answers prayers. Little did he know Michael was praying the opposite of him. At first, they did not see her but after 15 minutes, a beautiful car drove up and Mitsie came out. Unexpectedly, the driver was the elderly gentleman that was at Port Royal.

After the car left, Michael suggested that Marcia and Shawn hide in the car while he approached her pretending to be a prospective customer. He drove up and solicited her services, and she got in the car. They discussed prices for the various 'packages' available. Mitsie heard a shuffling and to her surprise, Marcia and Shawn. she tried to get out the car, but Michael had already accelerated. Marcia explained to the terrified Mitsie, that they are missionaries, and her brother wants to help her. Michael paid her for three hours if she promises to talk to them. She agreed. At the Hotel, Mitsie shared her story to a shocked trio.

CHAPTER 19

Time was not their greatest asset, so they knew they had to act quickly. Marcia was adamant that it would be akin to breaking the law of missionaries for them to leave Victory (Mitsie) in the state that she is in. Michael considered himself blessed; despite his condition, he had never experienced the atrocities Victory spoke of. With only hours before their departure, Michael contacted his father and asked if he had any contacts in Jamaica that could help them – they needed an escape for a seventeen-year-old young lady.

It was late but the two-hour drive to Pastor Amoy Singh's, Pastor Rory's friend, was worth it. Amoy's husband and children were visiting families in another part of the island and had not returned. She welcomed the travelers into her home and embraced Michael with more affection than the others. She later shared that while they were in Seminary studying, she and Michael's dad dated but after graduation, they drifted away due to distance and lack of communication. She longed for a son, but only had two daughters. Michael is the son she wishes she had.

She looked at Victory and love flowed from her eyes as she gave her a warm motherly embrace as she told her , "I love you Woman of Purpose and Victory." A sharp wail of anguish and pain startled her as the young lady clad in almost nothing hugged her back tightly. Michael explained that the young lady's name is Victory.

Amoy escorted Victory to the guest room where she would be staying . They then sat down, and Victory began to share her story. She lived in a low-income community where her older brother was involved in a gang. He was given a rifle to secure, and he lost it to a rival gang. They demanded payment for the lost gun, but the family could not pay. It was either the payment or the life of her brother. But then the gang leader suggested a third option – Victory could become their sex slave to pay off the debt. She didn't have much of a choice. She worked and paid off the debt. They still killed her brother and forced her to continue prostituting herself for them. She was trapped. The elderly gentleman she was with at Port Royal was her enforcer. He beat her whenever she tried to leave and threatened to kill her family.

Her family was able to leave the community under the watchful eyes of the local police who had received information that a hit was placed to eliminate the entire family. Everyone was accounted for except for Victory. She was listed as a missing person, but there didn't seem to be much effort to find her. Victory was passed around as a trophy to anyone who carried out important tasks assigned by the leader. She would have to spend the night with the gang members and whatever the desires of her owner were, she had to fulfill. This included but was not limited to violent sexual acts such as choking and beating and being urinated on.

She would also be given to non-gang member. Sometimes she was ordered to rob her clients and to sell them drugs. The worse one was the request from one called Darkness. He had a pet monkey and demanded that the monkey have sex with her. She reluctantly complied. It was brutally painful, and she received plenty bruises. He then requested that she do oral sex to the monkey. She refused and was beaten mercilessly. However, once she reported it to her enforcer, who informed the leader, Darkness was never seen again – he disappeared.

Victory revealed that there were several girls who were forced into a similar situation by the gang. The other girls were all addicted to crack cocaine. The gang induced and fed their addiction to keep them in submission. However, her enforcer secretly liked her and advised against doing drugs. He shielded her, but in turn, he had a personal hold on her. He literally owned her.

Moreover, Victory shared how about five months ago, she was tired of living. She thought it better to die than to continue living in this hell. She researched ways of committing suicide and decided on getting drunk and slitting her wrist. She bought two bottles of Hennessey and a razor blade and went to the seaside. She figured, if she got drunk, slit her wrist, and then fell into the water, her pain would not be severe. In a sense, she hoped the sea waves would wash away her existence.

She called her enforcer and told him thanks for looking out for her, and then informed him of her plans. To her surprise, he asked her what colors she wants to be buried in? It shook her hard.

As a drunk Victory slit her wrist, she heard a voice say, "Don't jump." She looked around but saw no one. The voice spoke again, "Help is on the way." She laid on the ground and soon persons gathered around and called 911. An ambulance rushed her to the hospital where she was treated. The doctors referred her to psychiatric evaluation and counselling, as well as prescribing medication for hallucinations because she said she heard a voice.

Unfortunately, it was time to leave for the airport. They gave Pastor Singh the monies they had pledge to offset Victories expenses. Shawn was delighted that she was at the pastor's house and allowed her to keep the phone and expressed his forgiveness. They exchanged numbers and promised to communicate. They hugged and eyebrows were raised- there was an obvious special connection present between them.

The rental car was returned, then they checked in and awaited their flight home. Moments before they boarded the flight, the hospital called giving an update; the baby was improving greatly, and they were grateful for the assistance rendered. Shawn asked if the mother called to give any updates, and he was told no. Michael explained, "While it is nice when persons show continued gratitude, some may not. But never allow that to prevent you from giving." The mother never called again.

CHAPTER

2

Shawn was excited to share with his mom and dad about his trip to Jamaica. He was surprised at their response to him losing his money and phone. They laughed him to tears. His phone was insured and Magrel had collected the replacement. He quickly removed himself from their presence and proceeded to his room. He eagerly wanted to hear from Victory.

Sam and Magrel repeatedly looked at each other suspiciously until Marcia asked, "What is it?" Sam replied, "Which do you want first – the bad or the good?" Michael answered, "The good." The good news was that the church leaders met and voted for the young couple to be ordained as missionaries of the church. They both were overjoyed at the surprising news. The bad news was that Grandpa Martin was terminally ill; He had stage four prostate cancer and the doctors only gave him five months to live. Both Sam and Magrel will be going to see him soon.

Back at work, Marcia was asked to lead a major law suite for the company. Sales had dropped drastically, and an investigation uncovered a manufacturer illegally using their label to service their clientele base. The matter was reported to the authorities and the company ordered closed. The case made the headlines, but Marcia could do without the public attention it was receiving.

One afternoon, as she was having tea, her phone rang and the words she heard angered her. A male voice said, "It is in your life's best interest to not proceed with the court case." Then the dial tone immediately came on. She had endured sexual bullying as a teenager, but now she refused to be financially bullied. She informed Sam, Michael, and the police. The police arrived and took her statement and her phone. They advised to increase the security at the home.

The following morning, she awoke to all her car tires slashed and her car sprayed painted with the words – *take heed missy.* She was scared. She stuttered and trembled as she tried to talk to Michael and the police on the phone. Sam and Magrel came rushing over and decided to give the case to another attorney, but Marcia rejected that offer. Sam insisted they outsource the attorney because they are unaware of who they are up against. Marcia was adamant that they should not back down and asked them to trust her. Unfortunately, these occurrences were leaked to the media, giving the case more unneeded spotlight.

Michael thanked Sam for insisting on the change. He was not prepared for his gift from God to be hurt. He suggested that they should take a vacation – spend some time with his father. However, they all knew that although that was a grand suggestion, the timing was off. Grandpa Martin was dying and needed his family close.

As Marcia pondered the recent events, she saw a beautiful face that she recognized walking towards her beside Shawn. "OMG, Victory! OMG, when did you arrive? Shawn, why did you keep this from me?" They hugged and hugged until their embrace was interrupted by the words, "Are you, ok?" That's when she realized, she had just experienced an open vision. She believes it was God's way of giving her the next assignment.

CHAPTER

2 1

Searching her bag as she tried to retrieve her ringing phone, Marcia found an unopened envelope. She would have to open it later. An excited Magrel was on the line, "Suzanna's water burst. We are on our way to the hospital now." Suzanna was not due until two more months. Her pregnancy had been challenging and her membranes ruptured at only 32 weeks gestation. Upon arrival at the hospital's maternity unit, she was immediately examined by the attending midwife. The findings of the examination revealed that she was in preterm labour as her cervix was already 5cm dilated. Upon review of her antenatal records, she had previously had five antenatal visits. She was known to be asthmatic with her last attack being three months ago. Her blood studies were done twice since pregnancy and same revealed that her hemoglobin levels were constantly below 9 g/dl despite being treated with iron supplementation. She was also positive for sickle cell trait and has been treated for pyelonephritis in pregnancy. As a consequence, she was referred to and seen twice in the high-risk clinic by the obstetric team.

In the labour and delivery room, an intravenous access was sited, blood was taken for further analysis and she was administered a 500mL bag of lactated ringer via the IV for hydration. She experienced excruciating pains and was advised to maintain bedrest to prevent cord prolapse from occurring. Four hours later her cervix was fully dilated and effaced and she progressed nicely into normal spontaneous vaginal delivery of a 1.5 kg baby boy. The baby had an APGAR score of 4 in one minute and then 5 in nine minutes and then 7 in ten minutes. The baby was cleaned, dried, swaddled and suctioned and then placed in an incubator to maintain warmth and also treated with oxygen therapy because he was experiencing severe respiratory distress.

To everyone's surprise she started complaining of experiencing severe contractions a second time. Upon examination it was noticed that another baby way coming. How could this be possible when her two ultrasounds revealed a single live intrauterine gestation? The baby almost spontaneously exited the birth canal but was noted to still be in the membranes and was descending in breech presentation. The membranes were ruptured artificially by the midwife and APGAR score was a perfect 10 in one minute. Immediately the midwife started calling her Miracle. She was cleaned and swaddled and allowed to bond with mommy, but her brother had to be transferred to neonatal intensive care unit for closer monitoring.

Before the mother could be transferred to the postnatal unit her blood results had returned and she was VDRL reactive which mean that she had tested positive for syphilis. Suzanna was in total disbelief. She was a faithful married woman, and was under the impression that Marcus was also faithful to her. All her previous blood studies came back normal, so this must have been a recent affair. She was sent spinning on a dizzying emotional roller coaster but was insistent on keeping it together for her newborns. The second baby was transferred to the neonatal intensive care unit and Suzanna to the postnatal ward. She was given a single intramuscular dose of 2.4 million units of benzathine penicillin G and released to go home the following day.

However, her house was no longer a home. Surprisingly, she did not explode with rage when she saw that man that she once called hubby. Instead, she was cold. She did not want anything to do with him. Every time he entered a room, she would make a quick exit. Previously, when they had disputes,

Suzanna would joke about kicking him out to the guest room. This time it was not a laughing matter when she asked him to sleep somewhere else. She made the bedroom her fortress and she would only leave it to get food or go visit her babies.

She visited the neonatal unit every day for two weeks to check-in and care for her babies. However, the nurses noticed that something was off with her. She was looking unkempt and unwell. Of note, she began to smell unpleasant as though she wasn't even taking a regular shower. The nurse reached out to her and suggested that she report back to the maternity unit and speak to the doctor there. After talking with her for a bit, the obstetrician diagnosed Suzanna with postpartum depression. He decided to readmit her to the obstetric unit and refer her to the mental health team for further assessment and management. A trusting relationship developed between her and the psychologist, Dr. Henry, as she began to open up about all the stressors in her life. On top of her list of stressors was the recent discovery that she had contracted syphilis. This could only mean that Marcus had cheated on her. Bitterness and confusion consumed her mind – should she confront him; she needed to but did not want to know why he would hurt her like that. She also had to consider how a divorce would affect her children. Dr. Henry did not feed her cookie-cutter answers, but rather assisted her in developing and employing effective coping skills. She was released within three weeks of being readmitted and she returned every week for another five weeks for outpatient review.

Both her bundles of joy, Laura, and Lucas were released to her after being admitted for two months. She also graduated from monthly to quarterly visits with the psychologist. After a year, Suzanna was given permission to discontinue her quarterly visits with Dr. Henry. They still decided to keep in touch, no longer as doctor and patient, but as friends.

Suzanna and Marcus' relationship had seen their ups and downs during the course of that year. Her initial coldness towards him thawed a bit as she witnessed how great a father he was to their babies. As a Christian, she knew that she was justified in divorcing him for infidelity, but she wanted to at least fight for her marriage. So, she finally confronted Marcus. She passed him the positive syphilis test results and commanded him, "explain!"

Oh my, I completely forgot about the letter, Marcia pondered about it the day after Suzanna's childbirth. She had no idea how and when the letter got into her bag, but the envelope was addressed to her, so she opened it and started reading it in her mind.

Dear Marcia,

I regret being the bearer of bad news, but I thought it necessary to share with you, since we have a mutual love. The family that you have been engrafted in, is not as perfect as you were led to believe. What they did for you, was more for them than you. You were used as them redeeming the family's name and prestige.

Sam's grandfather died of a broken heart. He started a business and when he was in his early sixties, like the prodigal son in the bible, his son, your adopted grandfather, stole his business from him. He asked for his inheritance and used it to become his father's competition. He reduced his profit margin, sold to his father's clients, and drove his father into bankruptcy.

I'm not reading anymore of this nonsense Marcia thought, but as she attempted to put the letter away, the pull to know more overpowered her and she continued.

The day of the funeral, your grandfather was not permitted to attend, and security guards were contracted to ensure that wish was not violated. Before his mother died, she vowed that the pain he caused his father will be multiplied unto him seven-fold. He sought redemption but she refused him. She died and blessed everyone except your grandfather.

He was adamant that he is going to be successful in spite of the curse that was spoken over his life. He worked hard, made a lot of shady deals, and joined a secret fraternity which ensured the success of its members businesses. This came with a hefty price – one of his children was sacrificed. The most painful for him was, he later found out that the child that he gave up, was the only one of the six children that was his. His wife had a secret relationship and all her children except one was for that man. They all resembled each other except that one. Your grandfather thought that that one was not his and found it easy to give him up as the price. He was tremendously heartbroken when the truth was revealed. The father of the children he raised as his own is the business partner who introduced him to the fraternity.

The business your father presently has taken over is cursed. As soon as his father dies, there will be a financial war between him and his siblings. As one of the business's attorneys you will be ushered into the middle of the dispute. There is one name that will be a surprise to everyone- Leroy. After discovering that his wife cheated, your grandfather had an extramarital affair from which, Leroy is the fruit. Before his mother passed two years ago, she told him about his father. He is presently discussing with his legal team regarding his inheritance from his father's business. He is rich and is not in need of money but revenge for being abandoned.

The fight that is brewing, will not be merely decided by the court but by the spirt realm…. Sam's conversion to Christianity caused his father to lose favor with the fraternity. It was seen as him not being able to rule his household well. To remain with them, he had to give an offering of twenty percent of his business. Presently, that percentage is not happy with monies being given to missions and charity. Should they win, all the financial support to the charity work in Bequia, will come to an immediate end.

Sam is unaware of what is coming and should not be privileged to this information as yet – he has a heart condition, which sees him wearing a metal plate. For the business to survive, there need to be a buyout of that twenty percent which will not be easy.

Magrel is no saint. Suzanna is not Sam's child, but he doesn't know. Although she and ex-husband were divorced, she loved him immensely. She expressed that to her counselor who advised her to stay away from him. After she got married to Sam she had a melt down and had a one-night affair with her ex. At first, she was unsure of who the father was but as the child grew, it became more apparent that the baby belonged to her ex.

Another secret Magrel will not want you to know, is the real reason why Andrea, her sister, had an affair with her ex-husband. Before her mother died, she wrote her Will and Testament, sharing everything she owned equally for her two girls. Magrel being the older, captured everything and then took care of Andrea. After her wrongs were uncovered, Andrea rebelled. She decided to take everything that was precious to her beloved sister.

Please forgive me, but it would not be Christian of me to not share about our mutual love. I am in love with your husband, and I promise you, we either share him or you lose him completely to me. I am a fair person and am willing to work out our terms of agreement. Be advised that I have information and pictures of you and David. No dear, not what you shared with your beloved family. I have the real dirt. You don't want to cross me. Take your time and process, investigate and conclude if the information shared is factual.

I will be in touch. By the way, ask Suzanna's husband who is Paris Lue from Barie.

P.S. You are welcome -Shalom.

CHAPTER

2 3

With letter in hand, Marcia sat perplexed in silence. She felt as though she was thrown out of an areophane without parachute. She had never thought they were perfect, but was all this true? Suddenly, an uncomfortable thought crossed her mind, was the writer a male or a female? What should she do? Marcia immediately decided to evade the urge to become angry or worry. Instead, she did what her grandmother taught her – pray .

After prayer she called Michael to come home immediately. Michael knew something was seriously wrong because of her tone and how she stuttered throughout her command. He had never heard her so shaken up before. Michael rushed home as quickly as he could, and accidently scraped the passenger seat fender as he navigated into the driveway. He took little notice of the damage, choosing to prioritize getting to his wife. As soon as they saw each other, they embraced. He could feel her trembling.

Marcia sternly questioned Michael, "Are you seeing someone?" His facial expression revealed confusion mixed with hurt. Rather than answering, he proceeded to release their hug and take slow steps away from her. She held onto his right hand and gave him the letter. After reading it, he had a better understanding of why she would ask such a question. So, he looked her straight in the face and gave her an answer, "This is crazy! No one can compel or bribe me into cheating on you. The love and sacrifice that you have made for us, will never be tainted by me. And no, I am not having an affair." Moreover, he suggested that they inform the police and their family immediately.

Marcia wanted to discuss it some more before they told anyone else. And her belly was beginning to rumble. They both laughed as Michael's belly joined in with a feline like growl. However, although they were both hungry and Michael prepared a scrumptious meal, neither had an appetite. So, they continued discussing at length the contents of the letter. The couple hoped that this was just a prank. Marcia commented on how she had never seen her father sick but noted that Suzanna did look different from Simone and Shawn. She also knew that Suzanna was going through a rough patch in her marriage, and prayed that the hint at Marcus' infidelity was not true

They talked until Marcia fell asleep on her husband's lap. He took her to bed and then prayed for her. He thanked God for her – she had loved him more than anyone. Then Michael realized he missed something, he looked back at the letter and zeroed in on the part that spoke about the real dirt. Was there something that his wife did not tell him? What was the real dirt between Marcia and David?

The thought of his wife withholding information from him was unnerving. The sleep that was near, suddenly vanished . He also started thinking about the time he found about Marcia's secret bank account. He went to Sam for advice. Sam told him it was common for married couples to have both joint and separate bank accounts. Michael relayed that it was not that she had a separate account, but rather that she hid it from him. She was the one who emphasized no secrets, yet she is guilty of same.

That night, Marcia tossed to and fro. She woke several times, and each time she got up, she woke her husband also. At 3:44am Michael was awoken by a scream of "No! No!" He held Marcia and comforted her. She said she had a dream where Sam was being drowned by an evil spirit and Magrel was bound and unable to help.

Michael voiced his opinion, "I believe we should really tell them about the letter."

The drive to her parent's home was without incident. On the way there, they prayed while worship songs played in the background. As they worshipped, they realized how much they missed singing together. They both agreed that they need to get back to doing music. Everyone was already there and waiting. Sam, Magrel, Simone, Shawn, Suzanna, Marcus, and the twins (Laura and Lucas) were all assembled.

Marcia began, "I have called this emergency family meeting because of a letter I saw in my bag. I don't know who placed it there, or how long it has been there. Before I disclosed the content, I pray that we will never allow anything or anyone to come between us. The enemy comes to steal, kill, and destroy. We are stronger when we are together. The concern on each face present, grew as she continued. No human is without errors, therefore let us not judge each other but rather if the contents are true, let us pursue redemption and forgiveness."

The meeting was interrupted by a phone ringing, It was Marcia's. "Hello" she said. A male voice on the other end responded, "Did you not read the letter? Sam is not healthy, if he dies, it's on your conscience. I know everything you do; you are being monitored. Remember, you don't want to cross me."

The phone crashing against the wall startled everyone. This was followed by the shout, "Why God, why?" Sam held her and enquired about what was wrong, but before Marcia could answer, Sam's phone rang. It was his pastor, so Sam chose to pick up. Pastor Paul asked to be put on loudspeaker and calmly addressed the family as if he knew they were all there. "Good day everyone. Sam, there is a spiritual war that has been unleashed against your family, if you are not careful, you will lose your family, your business, and your health. You all must sacrifice three days of complete fasting. At the end of it, God says, you will know what to do. Also, Marcia, do not read the letter."

CHAPTER

2 4

Magrel kept visualizing the last meal that they had before the fast started – barbecued chicken breast, potato salad with steamed vegetable. She had an unnatural desire to eat; she had fasted before but had never experienced this sensation. "God please help me! My body is shaking, I can't do this," cried Magrel. "Lord, I repent for all the food that we have wasted and the hungry that we have not helped." A resounding, "Amen!" came from Sam who then encouraged her to not give up; he reminded her they only had one more day to completion.

Across from Magrel and Sam, laid Marcia looking as though she had just completed a boxing match; she had the desire to be spiritually fulfilled; but physically it was too much. Marcia felt like she was forced into a hunger strike and she wanted out. Suzanna was concerned whether fasting would affect her ability to breastfeed. Her physician recommended intermittent fasting, and she made sure to not eat in the house. Marcus wasn't sure why the entire family was called to fast, but he knew he definitely had somethings to fast about.

On the second day of the fast, Pastor Paul entered the fasting room belting praises and singing the hymn, 'Come ye Disconsolate' and soon all of them in the room joined in. Praising God was more than medicine to the weary souls; they now felt like giants refreshed with new wine, they did not verbalize it but a newfound conviction permeated the atmosphere. They had to achieve the objective.

Going into the fast, they all agreed to make camp at the family house, which meant, no one would leave until the three days were completed. On the very first day, Pastor Paul joined them to worship and pray. Simone and Shawn had tiptoed out of the room when everyone had their eyes closed. They had snuck out to partake of forbidden delicacies – Simone had a bite of her favourite oatmeal cookie, and Shawn had donuts and a glass of milk. Once they had returned, they kept pacing the floor; they felt so guilty they had to come clean.

So, on the second day of the fast, as the family sat feasting on the song and the encouraging words shared by pastor, it struck a chord with all of them when Pastor Paul spoke on the importance of being quick to confess and repent. Each had their own conviction, they searched their spirits, they contemplated on their secrets and asked if hiding things was worth it? Should they share what they had done? How would such secrets hurt the others? "I cannot do this anymore!" yelled Magrel. With jittery palms and teary eyes, she looked as though someone had doused her with a bucket of water. "Family do not judge me" she stuttered between words, and after a long pause she continued "I have something to share with you." However, before she could mutter another word, the telephone disrupted the calm that had now gripped the room.

It was a message from Michael's father which read, "He that has begun a good work in you is faithful to bring it to the day of completion and be slow to speak and quick to listen". Everyone laughed then rejoiced having heard the readings. "God is truly among us and is helping us to complete what we have started, Michael commented. Magrel realized that what she was about to say was not a conversation to be had in front of everyone.

She would go on to sit down with Sam and Suzanna in private and confess her past transgressions and beg for their forgiveness. Sam touched his chest, as the news made his heart skip a beat. Suzanna was speechless. There was a long awkward silence, until Sam spoke up, "I forgive you Magrel," and turning to look at Suzanna, he told her, "You are my beautiful daughter, and I love you."

Suzanna hugged her mom and dad. She could not help but thank God for answering her prayers. She had asked God to reveal all secrets concerning her. Although she had confronted Marcus about his infidelity a few months ago but had never actually given him the opportunity to talk about it. Suzanna had determined to live with him for the sake of her children, but she was struggling to forgive him. Just earlier that day, Marcus had approached her and revealed everything. He admitted to having had a brief affair with a co-worker by the name of Paris Lue. Marcus regretted breaking his wedding vows, as well as having backslidden in his faith. He had recommitted his walk with the Lord during this fast and wanted to mend and strengthen his relationship with Suzanna.

The family spent most of the second night of the fast reading and expounding the word of God. This was followed by prayers being made for specific topics. Marcia was charged with praying for wisdom. When she finished the doorbell rang. Sam who was closest to the door, went and opened it. "Satan, the Lord rebuke you!" were the next words heard, followed by the slamming of the door. Everyone jumped to their feet and proceeded towards the door. A delivery lady from All Seasons Pizza Hut stood at the door with five large Pizzas. Someone had paid for the delivery.

After that incident, the house suddenly became extremely hot as though the air conditioning system was broken. Sam checked and it was working fine. Pastor Paul explained that the forces of darkness did not want the fast to continue. They held hands and formed a circle as they began to pray rebuking every evil spirit and thanking God for victory in Jesus' name. The temperature reverted to normalcy and was meted with ecstatic rejoicing.

Day three finally came. Michael and Shawn made it harder for themselves by constantly checking the time on the wall clock. Fasting was scheduled to be finished at six pm and they wanted to be eating by 6:01pm. Michael already decided what he would eat to break his fast. He was going to enjoy a big bowl of cornmeal porridge, bread, and fried plantains. Shawn said he wanted pizza, and they teased him about being the one to call for the pizza the day before.

Pastor Paul brought the group together to end the fast. He told them, "Lets remain focus. We have prayed, now let's worship and give God thanks." As they worshipped, a baby was heard crying from the bathroom. Laura and Lucas were peacefully sleeping in the room, so it wasn't them. They were all startled. Simone and Shawn drew closer to their father, and Pastor Paul went towards the sound. Then suddenly, the dishes in the kitchen all began rattling and the cabinet doors repeatedly flung opened then shut.

Although afraid, Shawn felt as though he received a revelation. He shouted, "It's my sister, my twin sister." He ran towards the bathroom, but his speed was terminated by the gripping hands of his father. Shawn pleaded, "Dad, she needs me, she needs us." Sam would not let him go, "Shawn, the crying you are hearing is not your sister; she is dead. An impersonating evil spirit is pretending to be her, to lure you to defeat." Shawn finally understood. He held his hero tightly.

Pastor Paul began speaking in unknown languages and projected his voice. He sounded like a military commander, "As servant of the Most High God, I take authority over this house and the very atmosphere, I declare that Jesus Christ is Lord and master. I command every evil spirit to vacate this house right now." Sam and Magrel joined in with "Amen," and "in the name of Jesus." The rattling and baby crying continued. Pastor Paul walked over to

Magrel and whispered something in her ears, and she nodded in agreement. He then went into the bathroom and closed the door behind him. His voice could still be heard but his words were muffled. Moments later, the crying ceased, and he alighted from the bathroom.

"Where is Michael?" Marcia asked. "He was right here with me, but now he is gone." Michael was found hiding in a closet. He recounted an incident that took place at his home church. Evil spirits invaded a congregant's home and possessed her daughter. They took the child to the local church and when they were casting out the demon, it looked at him and said – don't come near me or I will expose your secret. Since then, he had avoided any encounters with spirits. Pastor Paul made a mental note that he needs to do a series of teaching on demonology and the power of the believer through Jesus.

The rattling of the dishes increased, and water began flowing from the kitchen faucet. Pastor Paul encouraged them, "Come on soldiers, victory is ours. There is power in agreement." They all began to pray while Pastor Paul commanded the evil spirits to get out. Gradually, the rattling and the water flowing stopped and quietness was returned. They celebrated and Pastor Paul prayed a prayer of cleansing for the house. The ending of the fast was near and everyone was advised to pray for anything that they have need of.

As though the clock was removed from the room, Michael nor Shawn no longer looked in its direction. Everyone was extremely focused. Prayer and worship permeated the house. Magrel and Sam walked through the entire house praying. They recommitted their lives and rededicated the children to God. Marcia expressed that her faith in God had been renewed. She wants to do more for the Lord. In prayer she said, "I'm yours Lord, do what you desire with me." Simone cried as she witnessed the superior power of God. She declared, "No the power can defeat God's power." Pastor Paul repented for not having been a good shepherd. He had never taught the church about demonology nor how to destroy the works of Satan. Magrel told him to not be so hard on himself as he was their pastor for only three months.

"Listen," whispered Marcia to Michael, "do you hear Shawn's prayer?" Shawn continued praying unaware that they were paying special attention to his plea, "Lord, I really like Victory. She is beautiful, brilliant, and smart. If it is your will, I would love to marry her and have our own family. I have observed dad and mom, Marcia and Michael and they are happy. I know with their guidance we will be happy also. I thank you for impressing upon my family to care for her. I ask you to bless Pastor…. for taking her in her home and caring for her. If it is your will, can we have children? I don't want her to be childless like Marcia." Michael chuckled as he thought to himself, *who is to say that my wife will remain childless much longer.*

CHAPTER

2 5

66 Sam, I'm glad that you and Magrel are here. I will die if you don't help me. But it wouldn't be from prostate cancer. Please ignore what the doctors said; it's not real. Son, I made some poor decisions because I did not want to fail. Part of the success plan was, the way in which I would die, if

I should leave the fraternity. Of the nine options presented, I chose death by cancer.

This is a spiritual attack. If I walk away from Jesus and go back to their dictates, I will live. But I would prefer to die, than to lose my eternity with God."

Sam was speechless. During the fast, majority of what his dad told him was revealed to him but hearing it from his dad was still shocking news. In addition, they received instruction that his father must repent and destroy everything associated with the fraternity's sorcery. Grandpa Martin had to burn the parchment paper with his deceased son's name on it as well as the two watchers that he buried at the entrance of the businesses. Moreover, he had to redeem the part of the business that he gave away for twice its value.

Sam's father nodded in agreement to everything that was said. He apologized and both men, knelt down and repented. During their time of repentance, Grandpa Martin started vomiting. Sam panicked and called his pastor, who explained that it was a sign of being set free from spiritual bondage. Sam's mom heard the vomiting and came running. Sam explained the prayer of repentance and deliverance. She then knelt and repented in silence. Her husband told her, "You don't need to be quiet; I already forgave you." Sam was curious but kept silent. Suddenly two John Crows pitched on the two gate columns and Grandpa Martin declared solemnly, "They have come for me."

As the words exited his father's mouth, Sam resumed praying. "Father in the name of Jesus, we have committed to do all that you have commanded. Now, God, show yourself mighty, in Jesus' name." Approximately 45 seconds later on of the crow fell to the ground dead and the other flew away staggeringly.

Grandfather's breathing resumed to normalcy from the difficulty he had suddenly started having. The pain in his back and legs also miraculously vanished. They celebrated with tears of joy, warm hugs and passionate prayer.

That same afternoon, Michael's scream shattered the quietness that rested over his home. He had gone out for a quick trip to the pharmacy to get a refill of the pills that Dr. Ismalik had prescribed him. and returned to find his wife laying on the floor nonresponsive. "No God, no! Why, God Why?" He pleaded with God to heal his wife as he dialed the 911 operator. The EMTs found Michael beside his wife still praying for her.

After being resuscitated, Marcia reported that she answered her phone and felt as though someone hit her on her forehead. Then she knew she was on the ground and wanted to move but couldn't. She started praying, "Lord, don't let me die, but let mine enemies die." The doctors examined her and on finding nothing wrong with her they release her without medication.

Michael telephoned Magrel in a bid to inform her of what transpired with his wife. He discovered that around the same time Marcia was hurt, two ominous crows visited Grandpa Martin and died. Grandpa

Martin inferred that the two crows represented two lives – his and Marcia's. *Why me* Marcia pondered, *was it because I read the letter?*

Sam and his father followed all the directions of God. Surprisingly, Sam was able to easily buy back the percentage of the company that his dad had given up. The driveway of the business was dug up and the 'watcher' vials were removed and destroyed. "Sam," an exhausted Mr. Martin called as he sat down to rest, "God has given you time by sparing my life. But whenever I die, you have one more trouble to be concerned about – Leroy. He wants the business." By now Mr. Martin had already told Sam that he was not his biological son, and that he had Leroy outside of wedlock. Sam was not too concerned about the business because he had his built his own successful trucking business. And more importantly, Sam had learned to trust in God to fight the battles that were too string for him.

CHAPTER

2 6

Marcia could recall her conversation with Dr. Ismalik at the hospital as if it had happened the day before.

"Dr. Ismalik," she interrupted, "I remember categorically enquiring if there were anything that we should be concerned about, and you said no. Yet we are here today, with Michael in recovery and I'm here confused." Dr Ismalik did not address her rattling, but rather requested, "please tell me what happened." He sat beside her. Marcia shot back, "What happened? You caused me significant disappointments! You gave us all clear for penal penetration and we followed your instructions. But rather than us celebrating, here we are at the hospital. My husband is in pain, and I am fed up and unsatisfied. The penis we paid so much money for, broke at its inaugural service. That's what happened! Do you understand how devastating this is?" Marcia continued, "We have been having a rough marriage and the penis you sold us, was to be our marital saviour, but instead, you have pushed us to a worse place."

Dr. Ismalik listened and although he wanted to interject, he kept quiet. After she paused for almost a minute, she said, "What do you have to say now Dr. Bionic?" As he was about to speak, she assaulted him with more words. "Do you know because of your promise, my husband threw out my dildo? You took everything away from me, everything." Marcia's sobbing was met with a gentle hug from a nurse who was beckoned by the silent doctor.

Dr. Ismalik seized the opportunity to speak and apologized for her pain and disappointments incurred. He assured her, "Based on what we have analyzed so far, your husband will be ok. He is presently asleep but should be awoken in three hours' time. It seems too much pressure was levied on it too quickly – it needed time to climatize. Nevertheless, as a Christian, you know that good things come out of a bad situation."

After what seemed like an eternity, Marcia was invited to see her awoken husband. His smile radiated love for her as she entered the room. The gentle squeeze of her hand spoke volume and determination. "It's like" he said, "I appreciate you, we are going to make it". She kissed him on his forehead and assured him, "it is well."

All was not well. Marcia had consented to remove his bionic penis. The thought of living without a penis again crushed him. But then he received the best news he could possibly hear, "Michael, there is a possibility of your actual penis still growing…" He was incredulous. Dr. Ismalik gave a rather lengthy explanation using medical jargon that sounded like a foreign language to Michael and Marcia. He concluded by saying, "During the removal of the bionic penis we discovered an area which is usually self-opened as the fetus develops, that unfortunately remained closed. You have the option of opening that region and taking penis growth promoting hormones, or having the bionic implant reattached. Either option you choose, you will have to wait two weeks to do the operation."

Marcia and Michael took a week to pray on it and decided to opt for the operation to have Michael's penis have the chance to grow. After the operation, Michael had his doubts. *What if his penis didn't grow because he was a girl?* Such thoughts led him to going in for an unscheduled appointment with his counselor and skipping his date with Marcia, only to end up in a shoot-out situation.

Dr. Ismalik had told them that he should start seeing growth within eight weeks. During that waiting time, the family experienced a lot of drama. High stress situations like the ones that they had been experiencing, raised the sexual tension between Marcia and Michael. They utilized the dildo to have sex even after Michael's penis showed sign of growth. Dr. Ismalik had advised them to wait until Michael had experienced nocturnal penile tumescence (NPT), commonly known as morning wood.

And that time had come. Marcia awoke that glorious morning to see the sheets protruding upwards from Michael's groin area. She quickly ducked under the sheets and confirmed that he was indeed erect. Marcia screamed out in joy, waking Michael. At first, he was concerned, but it quickly dawned on him why Marcia was shouting, and he joined in making a joyful noise. They wanted to get busy as soon as possible. But before that, they had a time of devotion with God where they spent time reading the bible, praying, and worshipping. Michael prayed, "Thank you God for my penis!"

Afterwards, they had sex in a bath filled with water. Both Marcia and Michael reached an orgasmic climax. This was the best sex that Marcia had ever had in her life. Not even the spiritualist from her teenage years had come close to making her feel as good as Michael's real penis did. They did not understand why God allowed them to go through all that they did, but they were grateful that God had brought them together.

They had not revealed Michael's progress to their family as yet. Both of them wanted to make sure that the penis was fully functional before they told them anything. The first-person Michael called was his father, "Dad, I have a penis! I have a penis"

ABOUT THE AUTHOR

Jamaican born, Rev. Leostone Peron Morrison, is the author of several books, Mind Renewal: Biblical Secrets to a Better You, from which the devotional series was birthed, Mind Renewal 30 Days Devotional, Cross Over, Marital Intimacy, Marriage Reconstruction and Mind Colonization. He has served as an Assistant Pastor and Guidance Counselor at the Ministry of Education in Jamaica, as well as Probation Officer in St Kitts and Nevis.

Rev. Morrison is the founder of Restoration of the Breach International Ministry, of which the Restoration of the Breach School hosted on the Thinkific platform is a subsidiary. He is the founder of Next Level Let's Climb Bible Study Ministry. Bathroom cleaning was his first ministry assignment.

He is a graduate of the Jamaica Theological Seminary and holds a bachelor's degree in Theology, with a minor in Guidance and Counseling. He acquired a diploma in Biblical Principles from Victory Bible School, and a certificate from the International Accelerated Missions School. Rev. Morrison is married and has four sons and one daughter.

NOTE: For feedback, consultation or speaking engagements contact Rev. Morrison at restorativeauthor@gmail.com.

www.ingramcontent.com/pod-product-compliance
Lightning Source LLC
Chambersburg PA
CBHW050657290626
47170CB00015B/1593